Summer with Sunil

Summer with Sunil

ALISON LISTER

JAMES LORIMER & COMPANY LTD., PUBLISHERS
TORONTO

James Lorimer & Company Ltd., Publishers acknowledges funding support from the Ontario Arts Council (OAC), an agency of the Government of Ontario. We acknowledge the support of the Canada Council for the Arts. This project has been made possible in part by the Government of Canada and with the support of Ontario Creates.

Cover design: Tyler Cleroux
Cover image: Sofia Sciortino

Library and Archives Canada Cataloguing in Publication

Title: Summer with Sunil / Alison Lister.
Names: Lister, Alison (Alison E.), author.
Series: RealLove.
Description: Series statement: Real love
Identifiers: Canadiana (print) 20240335031 | Canadiana (ebook) 20240335066 | ISBN 9781459419292 (hardcover) | ISBN 9781459419285 (softcover) | ISBN 9781459419308 (EPUB)
Subjects: LCGFT: Romance fiction. | LCGFT: Novels.
Classification: LCC PS8623.I86 S86 2024 | DDC jC813/.6—dc23

Published by:
James Lorimer &
Company Ltd., Publishers
117 Peter Street, Suite 304
Toronto, ON, Canada
M5V 0M3
www.lorimer.ca

Distributed in Canada by:
Formac Lorimer Books
5502 Atlantic Street
Halifax, NS, Canada
B3H 1G4
www.formaclorimerbooks.ca

Distributed in the US by:
Lerner Publisher Services
241 1st Ave. N.
Minneapolis, MN, USA
55401
www.lernerbooks.com

Printed and bound in Canada.

To my partner, Greg, for being my rock and for helping me to take things less seriously.

01 *The Trip*

"CAN WE STOP SOON? I need to use the bathroom," I asked, looking up from my paused music playlist at the trees flashing by the window.

"Sure. I'll stop at the next comfort station," my dad said. "Should be in about ten minutes."

"Thanks."

It would have been handy, on a road trip, to have been born cis-male so that I could have pissed almost anywhere. Granted, you had to have the right attitude to stand and let it go at the side of the road.

We were on our way to Liverpool, Nova Scotia. My mom and dad and me. My older sister got to stay home.

The comfort station was crowded, with two ladies waiting outside the women's washroom, looking impatient and annoyed. I hitched up my baggy, low-rider, cargo pants as I passed them, and opened the door to the men's. It was empty except for a strong stench of urine, which I happily put up with in the interest of being able to piss right away and use a washroom that aligned with my gender.

While I sat for a piss — again, an inconvenience of my situation — I stared at my beat-up black and white sneakers, and wondered if I would still be functional by the time we made it to Liverpool. Going on seven hours stuck in a car with only my parents as companions was getting a little old, and there was still another hour until the hotel, and another eight hours to get through tomorrow.

One of the ladies was still waiting outside the

women's washroom when I left the men's. She gave me a less-than-friendly look, so I gave her a big fat smile and snapped my gum. *Don't try to police my bathroom choices, lady. You won't like what you get.* Besides, there was no way she could tell I hadn't been born with a penis unless she asked to look in my pants. At which point I'd report her to the owner of the gas station.

She didn't say anything, just turned back to the door of the women's toilet. I sauntered back to the car and got in.

"I guess I shouldn't have drunk that entire bottle of Coke," I said.

"I warned you," my mom said, but she smiled. "Road trip snacks. I get it. But you've got to think of the possible results."

"Yeah, yeah."

"Hey, Dominic," my dad said, "You know, we could go whale watching if you want?"

Huh. "Yeah? That would be cool."

"Once we get to town, I'll look up some places." He turned to my mom. "Is that something you'd do,

Doreen?"

"Sure. As long as there's a bathroom on the boat," she said.

The rest of the drive passed uneventfully. I stopped drinking pop and sipped from my water bottle, with fewer potty stops the happy result.

★★★

The tiny little town of Liverpool — Port of the Privateers — was a minuscule but picturesque town on the southern coast of Nova Scotia. Beautiful and peaceful, sure. But at sixteen and only six weeks away from my seventeenth birthday, I was more interested in hanging out with my friends than being a tourist. Unfortunately, all my friends were back home in Ottawa.

I flipped the page of my sketchbook and did some shading on something I'd been working on for over a week now. It was a side profile of my friend, Bashar. I couldn't seem to get his hair just right. He wore it in a retro style and for some reason, every time I tried to draw him, he ended up looking like Elvis. I looked harder at the photo that I was using as a guide, to see what I was missing.

I should have been happy that the long drive to get here was over. Maybe I was, but not that thrilled to have made it to our destination. We were going to be here all summer, and I didn't know how I was going to handle it.

My mom said my grandmother had loved growing up in this little town with Summerside Beach fifteen minutes away by car, but by the time she had hit her teen years, she had been desperate to leave. She didn't like that everyone had known everyone else's business. She'd wanted to go to university in Halifax, but her father, my great-grandfather, hadn't supported that because she was his daughter and not his son. So, she'd gone to Mount Allison instead, to get a secretarial diploma. Then she found a job at the hospital in Halifax, which was where she'd met my grandfather, who'd come all the way from England for a job as a doctor at the same hospital. After they got married, they had a home in Halifax, and later moved to Ottawa.

They were gone now, buried in a pretty cemetery between Ottawa and Manotick. I'd bet that cemetery was busier right now than this tiny little town.

I rolled onto my back and stared at the slanted ceiling of the room at the back of the upstairs. It wasn't very big, but at least it was mine. The window looked out over the backyard, but all I could see were trees and bushes. My parents had the main bedroom, of course. My older sister had decided to stay in Ottawa with her best friend, mostly because she had a full-time job during the months she had off from her studies at Carleton University, but also because she'd known that spending an entire summer here would be torture.

In two weeks, we were going to leave this rental and check into a small cottage that overlooked Summerside Beach. It was part of the Sand Dunes Beach Resort and Restaurant. My mom had wanted to rent it for all of July and August but they didn't have any available cottages for the first two weeks of July, so we had reserved this place instead. I wasn't sure which was worse, honestly. Maybe it was motivation to make sure I had a job next summer, so I could stay in Ottawa. Travelling with my parents was not as much fun as it used to be when I was younger.

"Dominic? We're going to the pizza place on Main Street for supper in fifteen minutes, okay?" my mom shouted from downstairs.

Ugh. Well, *pizza*. That was a positive. Because I was starving.

"Yeah. I'll be down in a minute."

I dug a pair of Bermuda shorts out of my suitcase and put them on, then grabbed one of my many black short-sleeved shirts and a red plaid button-down in case I got chills from the air conditioning. I may not have been the most fashionable person but I looked okay, and at least my clothes were clean.

I went into the tiny bathroom with my tube of styling gel and carded some into my light-brown shagged hair, making it look artfully messed up. Or, at least, I hoped that was the effect it had. My cowlick swooped dramatically in the front. I'd stopped trying to fight it because I wanted to put as little effort into my appearance as possible. The pale skin of my face was at least a little rosy over my cheekbones, and its spattering of freckles and sharp blue eyes, was okay, I guessed. My mouth was maybe a little bit big for my face, but my mom said my smile could charm the pants off people so I guess I didn't mind. It had gotten me out of trouble more than once.

"Is the pizza parlour air-conditioned?" I asked as I thumped down the creaky wooden stairs in my combat boots, holding the banister because the narrow staircase seemed a bit iffy.

"Oh, I don't know," my mom said. "Mark, do you know?"

My dad shook his head. "Do you want me to call?"

Both of the places we'd rented had air conditioning, because my mom had MS and the heat drained her energy and made her mild symptoms worse. She was on a long-term drug routine, so she wasn't disabled or anything, but she got tired easily and had to be careful not to do too much.

"No, no. It's fine," Mom said. "If it's really hot inside we can bring the pizza back here."

We walked along the sidewalk on Main Street. The town was pretty, there was no arguing that. Cute stores and gift shops lined the sidewalk. The main grocery store and a larger commercial area occupied space across the Mersey River. We'd stopped there to load up with supplies before driving into town.

The door of the pizza parlour jingled when we went inside, but nobody looked up. We grabbed a table near the window and the red-haired server came along without much delay.

"Hello! How are you folks?" she said.

"Good, thanks," my Mom said.

I nodded.

"Are you visiting Liverpool?" the server asked.

"Yes. We're staying at an Airbnb down the street," my dad said. "But Doreen's mom grew up here."

The server smiled at my mom. "Oh, you don't say?"

"Yes, she lived on Summer Street."

"How nice," she said in a cheerful voice, her Maritime twang obvious to my ears. She placed some menus on the table and told us she'd be back soon for drink orders.

"Dominic, do you think you could try to look a little more pleasant?" my mom said in a whisper.

"What?" I said.

My dad rolled his eyes. "Leave her alone, Doreen."

I bristled and opened my mouth to correct him for the hundredth time.

"Sorry," he said, holding up his hands. "Leave *him* alone. Look we're all tired and hungry."

"I'm sorry we dragged you away from your friends, Dominic. Isn't this a pretty town, though?"

"It's . . . nice. Sure."

"It's not Ottawa," my dad said. "Or Toronto. But it has its charm."

My mom watched me. She reached out for my hand. I didn't really want to respond, but I didn't want to ignore the gesture either. I gave it to her.

She squeezed my fingers. "You're going to have

fun, Dominic. I promise."

"Sure," I said, not really convinced. But my mom seemed so invested in me enjoying myself, I decided to squash my disappointment, at least for one evening, and try to be cheerful. I'd pretended to be happy for years, I supposed I could pretend again for one more summer. I didn't want to fake it, but I could.

It wasn't as hard once our food and drinks arrived. The pizza was hot with tons of cheese and pepperoni, and the cola was cold and refreshing, the caffeine giving me the lift I needed. My dad was right. It had been a long, tiring drive and we were all a bit grumpy. The food definitely helped. Afterward, I felt almost human again.

I watched the other people in the restaurant. They were mostly families, but there were three girls around my age sitting at another table who seemed all right. One of them kept glancing my way and I smiled at her. She ducked her head down and said something to one of the others. They erupted into giggles and I didn't know if they were making fun of me or just being silly.

Then I heard one of them say, "So many tourists." Another girl said, ". . . don't know why they come here." And someone else said, "Probably from Toronto."

I didn't mind being mistaken for someone from Toronto, honestly, but I got the impression they weren't exactly open to meeting new people. No-one made eye contact with me again and I ignored them after a while.

"Let's go to Fort Point Park," my mom suggested when she paid the bill. "I'm too tired to go out to the beach today, but we can see the ocean there."

Mom wanted to walk, but my dad persuaded her to let him drive us. It was only a twenty-minute walk, but the weather was hot and humid, and we didn't want her to overdo it.

We drove along the other end of Main Street. It was lined with historic houses and cottages, their lawns green and lush. At the end, it curved to the right and ended at Fort Point Park, a small stretch of grass and trees, with a couple of picnic tables, a stone monument, and two stationary cannons. A red and white, square-based lighthouse stood at the tip of the park where it looked out to the open sea at the mouth of the river.

We headed for the small parking lot beside the lighthouse.

The salt smell of the Atlantic Ocean hit me squarely in the face when I got out of the car.

"That's the sea all right," my dad joked.

The Atlantic Ocean opened up before us, vast and calm. We made our way along the concrete sidewalk that edged the greenspace and allowed visitors a clear view. On the other side of that huge stretch of water was England, which boggled my mind.

My mom lifted her chin to sniff the salt air, a blissful look on her face.

"When I was young, we'd come every summer. I loved it here. I'd climb on the cannons and go into the lighthouse. We'd sit here on the ledge with our legs hanging down, watching the horizon. It's so peaceful."

My dad put his arms around her waist and leaned in to whisper something in her ear. She giggled.

I decided to give them a moment to themselves, and walked a little further along the path, tying the sleeves of my plaid shirt around my waist.

I thought about my friends back home and what they might be doing tonight. I only noticed there was a person on the bench ahead when I was almost upon them. At first glance, I thought it was a girl. But as I got closer, even though this person was wearing a gauzy flowered skirt and white canvas runners, I couldn't be sure and I didn't want to assume anything.

I stopped near where they were sitting and crossed my arms over the viewing rail, pretending to look out to sea, when all I was doing was biding my time until I felt comfortable gazing at the stranger again. When I did, they were looking in a slightly different direction, giving me a view of their profile. A white cordless earbud nestled in the dusky shell of their ear, a new model iPhone in their hand, and a benign smile on their face.

As I watched, they turned towards me.

Soft brown eyes met mine, and I gazed back,

unblinking. They held me for a moment, then looked down at their phone and crossed one leg over the other in a casual but deliberate way. They looked at me again.

Their skin was the colour of burnished bronze, and their hair was a darker brown than their eyes, and hung almost to their shoulders in soft relaxed curls. A silver stud in their nostril gleamed in the sunshine.

The corners of their mouth tipped down as I continued to stare, and I realized my intense attention might be unwanted. It was hard to look away.

I turned back to the view, seeing nothing but my memory of how they looked, and those brown eyes gazing into mine and blinking slowly, like a cat. I watched the horizon, wondering how long I should wait before I chanced another glance. And took too long.

When I turned, they were gone from the bench and walking slowly away from me down the path. I watched their graceful and leisurely movements, and was surprised when they turned back and smiled at me.

My hand lifted of its own accord and gave a brief wave as if we already knew each other. They didn't return the gesture, but went on their way along the sidewalk with a feline grace.

I was breathless and dazed, as if I'd seen a ghost. But that had been a flesh and blood person, and suddenly, Liverpool, Nova Scotia, didn't seem so boring.

02 *The Siren*

I COULDN'T STOP THINKING about the person in the skirt I'd seen at Fort Point. It was as if they were some kind of siren, silently calling to me. I was convinced we'd had some kind of connection, as brief as our "meeting" had been. In such a small town, I was sure to see them again.

The next night, while my parents enjoyed a dinner together at Lane's Privateer Inn, I walked from our rented house to Fort Point Park, in case they were there again. I ambled the walkway three or four times, but there was no sign of them.

It was another gorgeous evening, so I sat on the bench where I'd seen them and wondered who they were. Did they live in town, or were they only visiting, like me? Or did they live nearby and only come into the town on occasion?

The odds were that I'd never see them again, but I didn't want to believe that.

Luckily, I'd thought to bring my sketchbook. I brought it out and concentrated on using my pencil to draw my view of the ocean and the wall and rail in front of me, as random people strolled by or stopped to look out to sea. I'd check to make sure they weren't the person I'd seen the other night, and then go back to my drawing.

When I was done, I flipped to another blank page. I started to sketch the face and body I remembered, but the details were vague. I focused on the eyes and hair, the delicate point of a chin, and the skirt and orange T-shirt. It was only a quick sketch.

I flipped the page and sketched the lighthouse, then on another page, the two cannons pointing out to sea. I couldn't deny that Liverpool was a sweet little town. But I missed my friends.

My parents were back when I got to the house, chilling in the living room. My dad had a show on. I said hi and went up to my room to call Bashar.

"Dominic! How's Liverpool?" he said when he picked up.

"Boring as hell. What am I missing there?"

He laughed. "Oh, not much. There's a party next week, though."

"Aw, man. You mean, one I'd want to go to if I were there?"

"Maybe."

"Huh." There were parties, and then there were safe spaces. They didn't always match up.

"Yeah, you know Carrie? She's having a few of us over for a barbecue."

"Oh, no way!"

I liked Carrie. And she was queer, so her party

would be safe *and* fun.

"How's the ocean?" Bashar asked.

I snorted. "Big."

"I guess."

"I did some sketches. I'll send you some photos," I said.

"That would be great. Things are all the same here. My job is annoying. I hate working late shifts."

"Well, you probably shouldn't be working at the cinema, then."

"What the hell else am I supposed to do?" Bashar said. "There aren't many places that want to hire kids our age. Which doesn't seem fair."

"It isn't. At all."

"I know, right? My mom said that back in her day, there were tons of jobs for teenagers. But things are different now."

"So different. So much worse."

Sometimes, it felt like *everything* was worse for my generation — the state of the planet, the price of . . . well, most things. I wasn't at all sure I'd ever make enough

　　　　SUMMER WITH SUNIL

money to move out of my parents' place, which was a depressing thought. Probably for them as well.

"Meh, I don't know. Could you imagine living without your phone?" Bashar went on.

"Not really. But maybe it was better not to be connected all the time," I said.

"I doubt it."

"Yeah, you're probably right." I laughed and kicked off my shoes, then lay back on the bed, staring at the ceiling.

"Look, I gotta go. I have to be at work in an hour," Bashar said.

"Sure, sure. Talk to you again soon, okay?"

"Sounds good. See ya."

I tapped to hang up, realizing that I wouldn't see Bashar until the last week of August, right before we started Grade Twelve. That seemed so very far away.

★★★

Liverpool was . . . interesting.

My mom was all over the little boutiques and

shops. My dad got a massive jug of beer from the local brewery and he was happy. We did some barbecuing at the house and ate out a handful of times.

I liked the restaurant at Lane's.

The Inn was a fixture in Liverpool. If my mom hadn't found the tiny Airbnb cottage off Main Street we would have stayed there, and I don't think I'd have minded. It was right across the bridge from Liverpool, giving it a great view of the town.

Lane's served fresh, local seafood and beef, and the bread was baked on-site. There was a bakery/café/bookstore/craft store at the other end of the building. The blueberry lemonade was to die for and their burgers were freaking awesome.

"So, Dominic, how are you liking the trip so far?" my dad asked, digging into his clam chowder.

I shrugged. "It's fine."

"Fine?" my mom said. "Is that all?"

I didn't know what to say. I didn't want to hate on the town she loved, but it wasn't exactly my idea of an exciting getaway.

My dad laughed, though. "It'll be better once we're on the beach."

"Yes!" my mom said. "You've been there before but you were younger. The view of the ocean from Summerside Beach is incredible. The white sand is so soft. I used to hang out there all the time when my parents brought me here on vacation. There's nothing better than lying on the beach in the sun, with a good book, and listening to the sound of the waves." She sighed and gave my dad a dreamy look.

I doubted that was exactly my dad's idea of a great time. It definitely wasn't mine. I was really starting to miss my gaming system. Thank god I'd brought my handheld. It was the only thing keeping me going.

"Have you texted your sister?" my dad asked out of the blue.

"Uh, no. Why would I?" I said. It was a legitimate question. I loved my sister, but we didn't really hang out or anything. She hadn't texted me.

My mom gave me a disapproving look. "Because she's your sister?"

Oh my god. "What am I supposed to text her?"

"I don't know, maybe ask her how things are going?" Mom said.

"But . . ." I scrunched up my face in confusion. "Don't you guys ask her stuff like that?"

My mom glanced at my dad as if she needed confirmation that I was not getting it and it wasn't just her. She levelled her gaze at me. "Lori might say things to you that she wouldn't say to us."

I blinked. "So basically, you want me to text her so you can find out what she's doing and if she's doing anything sketchy?"

"Well," my mom said, looking guilty. "When you put it like that, never mind. It's probably better that I don't know."

My dad looked a bit green. It was the first time they'd left Lori for such a long time and I could tell they were nervous.

"Look, Lori's not like that. I'm sure she's not getting into trouble," I said.

My parents exchanged a look.

"Well, at least you're here under our watchful eye," my mom said with an exaggerated leer.

"Yeah. Kill me now."

She smiled, as if my despair was a parental rite of passage.

03 *You*

BY THE TIME WE PACKED UP and checked out of our Main Street Airbnb, I'd given up on seeing the mysterious stranger. The Lighthouse route snaked along the coast toward Hunt's Point and Summerside Centre, giving us charming scenery as my mom drove, a selection of Maritime songs playing through the speakers. She was really getting into this vacation and I guess I couldn't blame her.

Eventually, signs for the Sand Dunes Resort, and

then the place itself, came into view. A two-storey, shingle-sided restaurant overlooked the rocky left hook of Summerside Beach, and a line of cottages and apartments faced the surf.

My parents had reserved a two-bedroom, beach-facing cottage. The secondary bedroom had twin beds, and doors out to the balcony shared with the main bedroom that looked onto the ocean. It was a much better view than the trees in the back of Main Street so I was happier here. I listened to the rhythmical sounds of the ocean while I lounged on the extra bed in my room, daydreaming about the stranger I'd seen at Fort Point.

I wondered who they were and what they'd thought of me, or if they'd thought anything about me at all. I thought I'd seen *something* in that serene, brown-eyed gaze, but I could have been mistaken.

I spent the first two days on Summerside Beach holed up in my room, reading one of the books I'd brought with me and trying to forget about the person I'd seen in town. I doubted I'd ever see them again, and the thought made me sad and made me not want to go out and do things. Because what if this happened all the time? What if all I ever got were glimpses of potential, and all I was ever left with were memories of something that might have been. Or maybe I was obsessing over something completely silly because we hadn't even said "hi." It was entirely possible that this family getaway was starting to affect my mental health.

By the third day, I was bored and restless. My parents kept suggesting that I go for a walk or go with them on their sightseeing trips, but I kept putting them off. They'd go for a drive, or out on one of the nearby nature hikes, and I'd wander around the empty cottage with an aimlessness that kinda scared me.

I needed *something*. I just didn't know what it was.

On the fourth day, I decided enough was enough. I'd never meet anyone, or see anything interesting, if I stayed inside this tiny cottage, even with its fantastic views of the Atlantic. I was sick of only looking at life from the inside.

"I'm going for a walk," I said to my parents after supper.

"Oh, good!" my mom said.

"Finally," my dad muttered.

I rolled my eyes.

"Do you have your phone?" my mom asked.

"Yes, I have my phone. Don't worry. I'll be back in an hour."

"Okay," my dad said. "Have fun."

I wasn't sure if fun was my goal, but I gave him a salute and headed out the door onto the front porch. Seagulls flew in zigzags over the surf, cawing at each other and getting into tussles. They were amusing to watch. But I really needed to move.

I took a deep breath and turned, ready to head down to the sandy part of the beach.

I wasn't expecting to see another person standing in front of the cottage beside ours, looking out to sea. I *really* wasn't expecting to see the person from Fort Point Park, standing there, with their earbuds in, wearing a blousy, baby-blue tunic over tan capris, with brown Chelsea boots and work socks. As I gaped at them and my mind boggled at this unbelievable turn of events, they turned to look at me, and a smile formed on their face, which didn't portray the same shock that I felt. Almost as if they'd expected to see me here.

"Hi," they said, pulling one earbud out. "It's pretty, isn't it?"

I couldn't speak, but I did manage a shaky smile and a nod. They held my gaze with a curious, interested look. Finally, I managed to say, "Yeah."

But now what?

I continued. "I think I've seen you before. At Fort Point Park, a couple of weeks ago."

"Oh?"

"You don't remember me?" I ran a nervous hand through my hair. "I mean, you looked at me . . ."

"I remember you," they said.

They seemed perfectly relaxed about this turn of events, whereas my mind was spinning.

"I was just about to go for a . . . a walk," I said, sounding awkward to my own ears.

"Me too," they said. "We could go together if you want."

"Sure," I said. "Wait, are you staying at this cottage? The one right beside mine?"

They nodded. "Yeah."

"I looked everywhere for you. And now you're . . . here."

They raised their eyebrows, and their smile widened. "You looked everywhere? For me? Why?"

I blinked. *What do I say now?*

"I'm not a stalker," I laughed. Except, maybe I was.

They looked at me for a long moment and then nodded. "I'm not worried."

Was this happening? How was this even real? Had I fallen asleep in my twin bed and been lulled by the ocean's song? Was this beautiful stranger actually a mermaid or a siren, and about to lure me to my death?

They pulled out their other earbud and put them both in a case, shoving it into a pocket. Then with a look my way to make sure I was following, they headed out to the sand.

After a bit, once we were away from the resort cottages and closer to the water, they paused and turned, holding out their hand.

"I'm Sunil."

"Dominic," I said. "Good to meet you." I shook their hand.

My powers of speech had returned. I still couldn't believe that the person I'd tried so hard to find, had been right here all along, while I'd been moping in the cottage right beside theirs.

"Can I ask about your pronouns?" they said. "Mine are they/them."

"He/him," I said, pointing at my chest. So, I'd been right, but also unsure about their gender, so I'd already been using they/them in my head.

We walked along the grass in front of the line of cottages and then the building with the rented apartments, then down onto the sand of Summerside Beach. I kept glancing at Sunil, finding it hard to believe they had simply materialized.

"I'm . . . glad I found you," I said. Then gave a shy laugh. "I mean, there aren't a lot of . . ." I frowned. I'd planned to say "queer kids" but I didn't dare to assume anything.

I didn't have to worry, because apparently, Sunil could read my mind.

". . . gender-queer," they pointed to themselves, "and . . . trans-masc?" they asked with raised eyebrows.

I nodded. Wow, they got it. Part of me wished I could pass as a cis-guy. I was still trying to decide if I wanted to go on T at some point.

Sunil gave me a timid look, which was the first time they hadn't emanated pure courage. Their words had been sure and solid, though. They glanced at the gathering clouds. "You still want to walk? It might rain."

I shrugged. "So? Let's go."

04 The Jellyfish

SUNIL AND I WALKED ALONG the beach, them in their brown Chelsea boots and me in my black army surplus.

"I like your boots," Sunil said.

"Thanks. Yours are cool, too."

"I don't like going barefoot, even when it's hot."

"Well, that's something we have in common," I said.

My heart beat faster. Sunil had long, dark eyelashes and plump lips. Their brown hair was gathered behind their head in a little bun today, which made their features and eyes stand out. I noticed the shadow of light stubble on their dainty chin and jawline. They had a way of walking that was graceful and sinuous, that reminded me of a wild cat moving through the forest. Something told me Sunil could be fierce.

"So, you're staying in the cottage beside ours. With your parents?" I asked.

"Just one of them."

"Oh."

"I live with my mom in Toronto. I'm on vacation with my dad."

"Oh wow." A laugh bubbled up inside me and I couldn't stop it from coming out of my mouth.

Sunil gave me a look. "What's funny?"

"I'm sorry, I didn't mean to laugh. Just . . . I was so worried about being away from the city, and that the kids here wouldn't be like me. And you're even more urban than I am."

"Interesting. Where are you from?"

"Ottawa," I admitted.

I wished I could have said somewhere cool like Vancouver or Montreal.

They smiled. "Ah. Government town. 'The City that Fun Forgot.'"

They didn't say it in a mean way, and I guess I didn't mind. That was what most folks from Toronto, and maybe everywhere else in Canada, thought of my home city.

"It's not that bad."

"That's good."

"Toronto probably has more things to do, though," I added.

Sunil shrugged. "Yeah, I guess. More for the people who can drink and party, though. I'm only seventeen. You?"

"Sixteen, but I'll be seventeen in a few weeks. Two more years until we can drink legally in Ontario. Or buy weed." I stopped dead and gazed at them. "Wow, I'm just so glad you turned up."

"I must have made an impression on you."

"Yeah, you did."

"But I was only sitting on the bench. Being me."

"I know."

They blushed and seemed pleased, looking away toward the waves, where the sun shone through a break in the clouds and bounced off the swells.

I was glad to be walking the sand with Sunil, and not stuck inside the cottage listening to my parents argue about what TV show to watch. They'd been married almost twenty years and they fought over the stupidest shit. I think they loved each other. They said they did and that they were in it for the long haul.

"Oh. That creature was not so lucky," Sunil said, stopping and staring at a jellyfish on the sand.

The see-through flesh reminded me of gummy candy or clear Jell-O.

"Ick." I stretched my boot out and tapped the top of it, making it jiggle.

"Ew. The poor thing," Sunil said.

"It's dead. See? It's all dried out. But still jiggly." I gave it another little tap with the toe of my boot.

We walked on in silence, gazing at other

beachgoers and listening to the roar of the surf. It was nice. But the silence had become awkward and I wanted to fill it.

"Have you been to Nova Scotia before?" I asked.

They shook their head. "Nope. Have you?"

I nodded. "Yeah, but not since I was eight. I liked it more at that age than I do now."

"Yeah?"

"Yeah. Well, it is pretty. And the ocean is cool." I gestured at the expanse of water beside us. "I guess . . . I'm just more of a city kid at heart. This wide-open space feels like . . . too much, you know?"

They laughed. "Well, I love Toronto, mostly. Sometimes it can feel crowded."

"No kidding. You probably think Ottawa's barely a city."

Sunil shrugged. "I wouldn't really know. Do you like it there?"

"Yeah, sure. I mean, my friends are there."

They raised their eyebrows. "Sweetheart?"

My gaze flew to Sunil's. Were they using an

endearment? They watched me closely.

"I mean, do you have a romantic partner — a sweetheart?"

"Oh! No. No romantic . . . partners." I said what I always said when I announced my single status. "I have high standards."

"Hm. Same." They kicked at the sand and laughed. It sounded like wind chimes.

"Oh yeah? So, no romantic partner for you yet?"

"Not yet. I keep hoping."

My heart did a funny little flip.

We walked on. The clouds got darker and spits of rain began to batter us. The wind picked up and the waves got bigger.

"You want to head back?" they asked, glancing at the skies, then at me.

"Not really," I said, "but maybe we should."

We turned around but took our time walking back. The heavy rain held off until we were almost at the resort and then the skies opened up.

We ran for the cottages. Sunil grabbed my hand

and pulled me under an overhang by the apartments. They stared at me, not letting go.

"Maybe this vacation will be more fun than I thought," Sunil said, their fingers damp and warm in mine.

"Yeah," I breathed, mesmerized by the beauty of their brown eyes and dark skin. "Meet me tomorrow?" I blurted.

I didn't want to leave without ensuring that I'd see Sunil again.

"What time and where?" they asked, sliding their hand from mine.

"By the rocks, where we saw the jellyfish. After lunch. Like, around one?"

"Okay." Sunil dug their phone out of their pocket. "Here. Send yourself a text. Then we'll have each other's numbers."

I tapped in: *Sunil is pretty* and hit Send.

05 *The Bridge*

I WAS RESTLESS the next morning.

I twirled a pen between my fingers as I watched my mom do her injection. She'd been on a medication for her MS since I was little, and I was used to seeing her jab a needle under her skin every morning — when I wasn't sleeping in at least.

She had been diagnosed with the disease when I was four years old, and I remember how scared she had been when she hadn't been able to coordinate her fingers. I just remember her telling me that her hands weren't working properly, but that she was going to see a doctor to find out what was wrong. She pretended with me that everything would be fine, and even made jokes about not being able to carry her coffee without spilling it, but I'd heard her talking on the phone with my dad one time and crying, so I knew something was very wrong, even at that young age.

Her hands had gotten better, and she'd only had mild relapses ever since. Once she'd used a cane for a couple of weeks, for balance. But things had been good for a while and we all hoped they would continue to be.

Mom said we shouldn't worry about what might happen in the future. I don't know how she did it, to be honest, and sometimes I couldn't help thinking about the "what ifs."

"Honey, we're going to drive into town for lunch and some shopping," my mom said. "Do you want to come?"

"No thanks. I'll just hang around here."

"Okay. There's bread and cold meat in the fridge. And those pastries we bought the other day."

"Sounds good," I said from the sofa, where I was pretending to read. "Have fun."

I kept checking the time on my phone and wondering if I should send Sunil a text to remind them we were getting together. But that was probably overkill.

At noon, my phone dinged with a text from Sunil.

Sunil: dominic is handsome ☺

Dom: hi

Sunil: we still on for one

I couldn't help the grin that spread across my face.

I texted back.

Dom: yep

Sunil: by the rocks?

Dom: wonder if the jellyfish is still there

Sunil texted:

Sunil: you can jiggle it with your boot again

Why did that sound so dirty? I blushed and replied.

Dom: what if im wearing flip flops

Sunil: dont, i like the boots ☺

Well, well, well. My summer vacation had definitely become more interesting.

★★★

The jellyfish was gone. We stared at the place where it had been.

"Huh," Sunil said. "I wonder if someone took it."

"That would be a very big and smelly souvenir. Maybe some animal came and ate it."

Sunil made a grossed-out face. "Probably more likely."

"Nature's Jell-O."

"Oh my god. Gross."

We sat on the rocks, watching the waves. The beach was crowded today since the sun was out. There were hardly any clouds, and it was early in the afternoon.

Sunil was wearing black short shorts with a pink t-shirt. They had on a cropped, tan linen jacket with a colourful patch of an ice cream cone on it, and they were wearing their Chelsea boots again. They looked so adorably cute my breath had caught in my throat when I'd seen them. Their legs were as smooth as a dolphin's. They noticed me staring.

"I shave them," Sunil said.

I didn't know how to react. I liked the look of Sunil's smooth legs, and I'd bet they'd feel soft to the touch, but I didn't have a hate-on for body hair.

They continued. "I didn't for a long time because it seemed like such a pain. But, honestly, the first time's the worst. If you keep up with it, it's not that bad."

I looked down at my own legs, dusted with light-brown hair. I couldn't imagine spending the time to get rid of it.

"Come on," they said, jumping up from the rock and holding out their hand. "Let's go."

I didn't think twice. I took Sunil's hand and we set off down the beach.

Their skin was smooth and warm and their hand was relaxed in mine. I noticed a few people looking at us, but no aggressive stares or anything. After a bit, we let go and just walked beside each other.

At the farthest end of the beach, there was an old railroad bridge. Some kids were on top of it, and as we watched, one of them jumped off and into the water, making a big splash as the ones on the bridge cheered.

"That looks like fun," I said.

Sunil frowned. "Looks dangerous to me."

"Well, it's not like I want to *do* it."

The kids on top of the bridge laughed and shrieked. They seemed a lot younger than we were. We watched for a bit. Nobody died, so we turned and walked back along the beach. When we got close to the cottages again, Sunil turned and asked, "You want to go get ice cream?"

I pointed at their jacket. "I've got ice cream right here."

They grinned. "No, actual ice cream. There's a stand right by the highway. I'll show you." They took my hand again and pulled me toward the grassy dunes in the direction of the public parking lot.

It was a nice feeling, holding Sunil's hand. We

were friends, and there was no pressure to do anything but have fun and get ice cream. Although I did wonder what the smooth skin on their legs would feel like under my hand, or how nice it might be to snuggle up together on the couch.

But I didn't know if Sunil was interested in anything more than a friendship. Maybe I was naive and the hand-holding was their way of telling me they *were* interested in more. But on this beach, in this place, with the sun high in the sky, seagulls shrieking, and our parents close but far enough away, there didn't seem to be any kind of rush to do anything but enjoy the moment.

06 *Ice Cream*

SUNIL TOOK ME TO AN ICE CREAM STAND on the highway that was about a five-minute walk from the Summerside Centre parking lot. We walked along the pebbled edge of the two-lane highway until we spotted the brightly coloured van with the serving window and list of prices.

I offered to buy Sunil's ice cream and they let me. But then they offered to pay for mine, which was hilarious, so I let them. We touched the scoops on our waffle cones in a toast.

"To summer vacation," they said.

"To making new friends," I added. "And not hanging out with our parents."

They laughed. "Hear, hear."

We found some boulders to sit on and watched the cars go by.

"My dad's hooked up with some woman in town," Sunil said, making a face. "So, it's not like I can hang out with him anyway."

I must have looked confused.

"Very relaxed parenting style. Part of why they split," Sunil admitted. "I haven't told my mom, though. About the woman in Bridgewater."

"Oh." I didn't know what to say. "Wait, does that mean he isn't staying with you at the cottage?"

Sunil shrugged. "He pops in sometimes to make sure I'm not dead. And that I'm staying out of trouble. And drops off groceries." They waggled their eyebrows. "I could get into so much trouble."

I frowned. "Isn't he supposed to be on vacation

with you, though?"

Another shrug. "I thought that was the plan. I should have known. Can't really complain, though. What other seventeen-year-old gets their own luxury cottage overlooking the beach?"

To be honest, they didn't look that thrilled about it.

"I'm used to it," they said, giving me a smile that was supposed to be reassuring but was just kind of heartbreaking.

I couldn't imagine being stuck in a strange place without my parents around. I mean, I was glad they weren't crowding me, and that they let me do what I wanted. But to completely ignore me and not make any effort to ensure I was having a good time? When I'd had no choice but to come? I didn't think Sunil had had a choice, but maybe I was wrong.

I wasn't sure I wanted to ask them.

"You shouldn't be," I said quietly. "That's kind of messed up."

"It is what it is."

"How far away is Bridgewater? I thought you

meant he met someone in Liverpool."

"Nah, they met online." Sunil tapped a finger to their head. "He planned it."

God. That was even more messed up.

Sunil answered my question: "Bridgewater is the nearest city. It's about forty minutes from here."

"Damn."

"Yeah, I think he wanted to keep us as far apart as he could, but still be sort of nearby in case of any problems."

"I don't think forty minutes is all that close. I assumed you meant he was in Liverpool. How's the almond mocha?" I asked, changing the subject.

"So good," they said, licking a circle around the top of the giant scoop. I pretended not to watch their pink tongue glide over the frozen treat, but it was distracting and made me feel weird. Good weird. "How's the double chocolate?"

"Delicious. This is a cool spot." I gazed at my ice cream. "Literally."

"Yeah, I found it the day we arrived. I kind of

scoped out the neighbourhood after my dad stocked the fridge and took off. There are some benefits to being independent."

"I guess that's true."

When we were finished, we walked back to the beach.

"What do you want to do now?" I asked. "My parents are still in town, doing some shopping."

"Yeah?"

"You want to come over to my . . ." I made a fancy gesture. ". . . swanky beach cottage?"

"How could I refuse?"

I grinned. "You have one just like it, though."

"But that one doesn't have *you* in it."

I blinked, not sure what to say. They looked at me with an obvious and sincere affection that made me weak in the knees.

★★★

"We'd better take off our shoes," I said, "My mom will be pissed if she comes back to find sand all over."

"Sure," Sunil said, taking off their boots. Their socks were also ice cream-themed.

We put our boots on the mat and proceeded to the kitchen.

"Is this one the same layout as yours?" I asked.

Sunil looked around. "The paint colour's different. And the artwork. The rest is the same. Except yours looks more . . . lived in." They glanced at me. "I guess because there are three of you."

"Yeah," I said, feeling bad about Sunil's dad abandoning them. "And also, I tend to leave stuff everywhere," I added, tidying up the coffee table and taking my dirty mug into the kitchen.

"Well, you are on vacation. It's a good time to be lazy."

"True."

We stood at the kitchen counter, awkward now, when we'd been perfectly comfortable together on the beach and at the ice cream stand.

"We could watch TV," Sunil said. "I have the password for the streaming service memorized."

"Yeah, okay. Or, you know, I have a system in my room."

"No way? Cool."

"Yeah. We could play a video game . . ."

"Yeah, okay."

Turned out Sunil was an expert at most of the games I'd brought, and they beat my poor ass about six times before fifteen minutes was up.

"Holy shit, could you give me a break? Jesus."

They laughed. "You'll win the next one, probably."

"I don't know . . . you've got magic hands . . . or something."

They smiled and met my gaze, waggling their eyebrows, which made me laugh. "Oh, honey, my hands are more magical than you know."

The funny thing was, if some idiotic fuckboy from my school had said that, I'd have hated them. But from Sunil, who was clearly joking but also quite possibly not joking, it was hilarious and charming.

I held their gaze, thinking things that were not

exactly rated PG. But we were sitting on separate beds and holding controllers. There was no way I was going to make a move on Sunil the first time we hung out in private. I had more class than that.

We were friends, and barely that, but there did seem to be chemistry, and I had hope in my heart for more. I didn't know what it was about them, but they had drawn me in from the start.

07 The Explanations

SUNIL LEFT AFTER AN HOUR OR SO, with some excuse about not wanting to be here when my parents got back. I wasn't sure why, but I didn't question it.

I walked Sunil to the door and stood there while they pulled their boots back on and placed their hand on the screen door.

"That was fun," they said.

"Yeah."

"Maybe we can do something tomorrow?"

I grinned. "I'd like that."

"Unless your parents drag you sightseeing or something."

I didn't think they would — I usually had the choice to go with them or not — but I said, "If they do, I'm sure you could come with."

For a half-second they looked unsure and anxious but then they smiled and nodded. "Maybe."

"I'll text you in the morning. Not too early."

They shrugged. "I'm usually up by seven."

Good to know.

"Bye," they said and gave me a cute wave.

"Bye," I said.

The cottage felt empty and boring when they'd gone. It was weird to know they were alone next door.

"What did you get up to today, Dominic?" my mom asked over supper.

I had already wrestled with the question of whether or not to tell my parents about Sunil. If Sunil hadn't been staying in the cottage right next door I might have held off. But just in case my folks happened to see them, or see us together, I figured I might as well let them know I'd made a friend.

"Actually, I hung out with someone."

"Yeah?" my dad snapped his head up from gazing at his steak like it was going to bite him.

"Their name's Sunil. They're staying in the cottage next door."

"Oh. That's cool. A boy?" my mom asked.

I shook my head. "Sunil is gender-queer and uses they/them pronouns."

My dad nodded. "Oh."

"Well, I'm glad you've made a friend," Mom said. "I assume he's — I mean, *they* are — a nice person?"

"Yeah, obviously. You think I'd make friends with an asshole?"

"Language, Dominic," Dad said. "Come on."

"Sorry," I said, shaking my head. "Yeah, Sunil's great. They're cool."

"That's good," my dad said. "Don't get too

attached, though. You'll probably never see them again after we leave."

What the hell?

"Mark," my mom said.

Dad shrugged. "What? We're only here for the summer."

"That's a whole other month," I said. "That's a long time."

"To you maybe," Dad said. "To me my vacation is already half gone."

"Also, there's this thing called The Internet now, Dad. It's really cool, you should try it sometime."

"Cute. I know you kids can hang out on the Snapchat or Facebook but —"

"*Nobody* uses Facebook," I groaned.

"Well, I do," my mom said.

"Exactly," I replied.

"But you have a Facebook account!" she pointed out.

"That I never use, except when I'm tagged by you or someone else I'm related to. Trust me, kids my age don't use Facebook to connect with anyone other than family."

"What do kids your age use? Instagram?" my dad asked.

"Yeah, mostly. Some people use TikTok, but I'm not a fan."

"Huh," my dad said. "I'm sorry. I didn't mean to be insensitive."

"It's okay. Anyway, I really like Sunil and we're hanging out. For god's sake, if you happen to see them, please be nice. And not weird."

My parents exchanged a look. "We're never weird."

"Sure."

We ate in silence until my mom spoke up.

"Where is Sunil from?"

"Toronto," I said.

Dad and Mom exchanged another look.

I finished eating and excused myself, saying that I wanted to call Bashar.

Up in my room I texted Bashar to see if he was up

for a phone call. He called me back right away.

"Hey! How are things?" he asked.

"Oh, you know. Kinda boring. I'm seeing way too much of my parents," I said, lying down and staring at the ceiling fan.

"I bet!"

"But I, uh . . . I met this really cool person, though." Bashar could probably hear me smiling. Maybe he could hear me blushing.

"Yeah? Our age?"

"Yeah. They're staying in the cottage beside ours, with their dad."

"Cool, cool."

"Yeah, except apparently, their dad has a girlfriend in a city that's, like, forty minutes away and is hardly ever around. Stocks the fridge, though."

"No way. Kinda ideal, really."

"You think?"

"Hell, yeah. I'd give my left nut for a vacation like that."

"Yeah, you'd get into so much trouble." I laughed.

"Probably. So . . . what's this kid's name? And is he or she cute?"

"*They* are adorable."

"Oh, really? How fascinating! Do tell . . ."

"Well, they're cute as hell, and their name is Sunil. They have the most beautiful eyes and the sweetest smile."

"But you're not gonna tell me if they're a boy or — oh, wait. You mean *they* they?"

"Exactly."

Bashar laughed. "You didn't think you'd meet any queer kids in Nova Scotia."

"I know, right? Well, surprise, surprise."

"Do they care that their dad isn't supervising? Or are they having wild parties and orgies?"

"I think if they were partying right next door, we'd hear something. But I have no idea. We walked on the beach yesterday and today. It doesn't seem like they're looking for excitement. They're just vibing, you know? But I think they do mind that their dad has ditched them. And it must get lonely, right? I mean, my parents can be dicks sometimes, but I don't think I'd want to be out here by myself. Or, you know, it kind of shows their dad doesn't want to spend time with them."

"Yeah. That's gotta hurt."

"Right?" I remembered the sketch I'd finished the day before. "Oh, hey," I said, flipping the pages of my sketchbook back. "Look."

I turned my phone so Bashar could see the sketch I'd done.

"Is that me?"

"Yeah. Duh."

"Why do I look like Elvis?"

I closed my eyes and threw my sketchbook on the floor.

Good Coffee

THE NEXT MORNING, I got up early and went to sit on the patio with my sketchbook. Drawing was a good way to settle myself when I was antsy and excited.

This was a scenic spot, there was no denying that. My parents had paid a lot of money for this vacation, which was why I'd tried not to grumble too much about having to come with them. Maybe they would have preferred to leave me at home, but they had wanted to spend a summer with me since they knew

I was heading into my last year of high school, and next summer I'd be working — hopefully — so that I could contribute some money to my university tuition, wherever I decided to study. Yeah, that was a sobering thought. I still didn't know what I wanted to do or which school I wanted to go to. It was tempting to leave Ottawa, but so damned expensive. I'd probably stay out of sheer laziness.

I sat in the Muskoka chair and sketched what I saw. There was a small stretch of grass and then a concrete retaining wall that rose about a foot from the grass and stretched down several metres to the rocks on the beach below. Looking over that wall, it seemed like the sea was at your feet.

At the moment, with the sun coming up on another beautiful day, and the calm and peaceful ocean before me, I was glad I'd come.

I got lost in my sketching, so oblivious to reality that the familiar voice at my elbow startled me.

"Good morning."

My pencil skidded across the page.

"Shit," I said, gazing up at Sunil who had suddenly appeared. I had been so absorbed in my work that I didn't hear the door of the cottage open.

"Damn. Sorry!"

"It's okay."

"But I ruined your drawing."

I glanced at the page.

"Technically, I was the one who did that. And it's not ruined. I can always do it over."

They frowned.

"Sunil, it's fine."

That was when I noticed they were holding two mugs. "Is one of those for me?"

They smiled. "Coffee. I don't even know if you drink it but I brought you some."

I laughed. "Seriously, how old *are* you?"

"Old enough to drink coffee."

I reached for the cup they held out to me. "I'll try it."

"I put a ton of milk and sugar in it. It'll be sweet."

The mug looked like the ones we had in our

cupboard — a soft grey colour with the Sand Dunes logo on it. The coffee smelled good.

I got the feeling that Sunil had learned to do quite a lot on their own.

Sunil was the least put-together I'd ever seen them. They were wearing a pair of navy sweatpants and a *Stranger Things* T-shirt. Their hair was mussed as if they'd just got up. They had their boots on, though. I wondered if they had on cute socks again today.

I was in gym shorts and my unlaced combat boots, with some random soccer T-shirt I'd thrown on.

"What time is it?" I said, squinting at them.

"You really get into your sketching."

"Yeah."

"It's almost eight," Sunil answered my question. They took a sip of their coffee and motioned to mine. "Try it."

"Okay. You can sit down, you know. There's another chair."

"I'm okay."

"Ready to run?"

They cocked their head. "Huh?"

"Nothing." I tried the coffee. "Oh, this is actually good," I said, taking another sip.

"I don't think I could do without it now. I started having it regularly at fourteen. Probably not good for me, but you know, it's not heroin."

I laughed. "True."

Seriously, this kid was magical and so strange. But I loved every unexpected thing about them. Wait, I mean, I *liked* every unexpected thing. Who used the word love for a new friend? Not me. No sir. Never.

Sunil was sweet and cool and unique, and that was all. But that was a lot, too.

The sound of a screen door opening broke the silence and I closed my eyes, knowing what it meant.

"Oh, hi! You must be Sunil," my mom said.

Sunil looked panicked for a second.

I turned to my mom. "Yeah, this is the person I was telling you about."

Mom smiled and offered her hand to Sunil. She was in a pretty sundress and bare feet, her greying brown hair wet from the shower.

"Sunil, this is my mom," I said, with an apologetic smile.

Sunil had recovered from the shock of seeing a parental figure and shook my mom's hand. "Nice to meet you Mrs. —" Their gaze flashed to mine as we both realized we hadn't exchanged last names.

"Just call me Doreen. That's a great show," she said, nodding at Sunil's shirt. "Winona Ryder was a young movie star when I was your age. It's great to see her acting again."

Sunil nodded. My mom turned to me.

"Are you drinking coffee?" she asked.

"Yeah. Sunil made me some."

She gazed at Sunil. "Well, my goodness. That's such a nice gesture."

I could tell she was impressed, both at Sunil's ability to make a pot of coffee and at the fact they'd brought me a cup.

She turned back to me. "Your father's in the shower. But I saw you two and thought I'd come say hi."

We stood there awkwardly. My mom turned to me.

"Dominic, we're going to drive into Liverpool again today, if you and Sunil would like to come along. You don't have to hang out with us old folks but we'll take you both to lunch."

I glanced at Sunil and raised my eyebrows. It might be fun to get a drive into town and a free meal, and then we could go exploring on our own.

Sunil seemed caught off guard. "Oh . . . sure. I guess?"

I gave them a big smile and they seemed to relax.

"Well, ask your parents if it's okay — oh, I mean your dad, right? And if he says yes, then we'll probably head out around eleven."

"Okay," they said, gaze flashing to mine and then back to Mom's. "Thank you."

My mom went back inside.

I turned to Sunil. "You don't have to come if you'd rather not. But it would be cool if you did."

They gave me a genuinely pleased smile. "I would like to come."

I looked at my feet. "Yeah. I didn't tell them your dad wasn't around. They don't need to know that."

"Okay, good. I'd rather not have them worry or think I'm being neglected."

I gazed at them, wondering if *they* thought they were being neglected. I was pretty sure I did.

09 The Artist

SUNIL AND I SAT TOGETHER in the back seat of my parents' SUV, gazing out at the thick pines and glimpses of ocean and beaches along the twisty Lighthouse Route. Sunil had changed into white leggings and a gauzy blue skirt that skimmed their knees, and a purple tank top with the Capri-Sun logo on it. They had on a short-sleeved, sheer pink blouse, opened in front, as a light cover. I was in jean shorts and a *Mandalorian* T-shirt. Guess which one of us looked cuter?

That was a trick question.

"Oh, wait!" my mom said to my dad, who was driving. "I saw this sign yesterday — can we stop for fifteen minutes?"

"Sure."

"What is happening?" I asked, as my dad pulled the car off the two-lane highway onto a gravel drive.

Sunil pointed to a sign that said:

LOCAL ARTIST AND SCULPTING STUDIO,
*Please stop in! Open between 9:00
and 1:00 on weekdays and 11:00 to
6:00 p.m. on weekends.*

"Your mom wants to stop."

She turned to us with an apologetic smile. "Sorry. Just a small pit stop."

"Sure," Sunil said.

"Fine," I agreed.

We couldn't complain. We were getting a drive into town and I had big plans. Well, medium-sized plans, anyway.

We drove along the pebbled drive for at least a hundred metres until it passed by and curved around behind a grey clapboard cottage. There was a flat, grassy spot to park, and a sign saying, "Joss Whitby Artist," with paintings of tiny flowers all around the words.

As we pulled onto the grass and left the car, a middle-aged man in jeans, flip-flops, and a white button-up came out of the house and down the porch steps.

"Hiya! Welcome," he said as the screen door creaked and then shut behind him.

He wasn't bad looking for an older man and I liked his eyes.

"Hello!" my mother said. "We came to see the paintings and sculptures."

"Wonderful!" the man said, gazing at me and Sunil.

"Hi," I said, and Sunil gave a little wave.

"You're a little bit out of the way here," Dad said. "But it's a stellar spot."

"It is, isn't it? We like it here. It's quiet," he said, as another, younger man came out of the house and stood leaning against the porch railing.

"I'm Joss Whitby," the first man said, beckoning us further into his backyard.

"The artist! How nice to meet you," my mom said, primping and smiling.

I hoped Joss Whitby didn't see me rolling my eyes.

"This is my partner, Caleb Finch," Joss said, gesturing to the man on the porch. Caleb smiled and nodded, then crossed his arms over his chest.

I glanced at Sunil, whose gaze switched back and forth between Joss and Caleb with curiosity and interest.

"I love your skirt," Joss said to Sunil. "Here, come and see the sculptures." He ushered us toward the other side of the house.

We spent about half an hour following Joss Whitby around his garden, looking at his unique and whimsical creations. Then we went inside the small cottage and he showed us his many paintings, most of which were maritime landscapes of the local scenery. Caleb followed us at a discrete distance, pointing out one or two things Joss missed and explaining why he liked certain pieces.

"These are great," I said, pointing to a collection of paintings of the ocean shore. He used splashes of colour and shade in a way that was subtle but deliberate, to indicate motion and create interest.

My dad bought a sculpture that used driftwood and tin to create a humpback whale breaching the surf, and my mom bought a small painting of the lighthouse at Peggy's Cove.

"Dominic's an artist," Sunil said, gesturing to me while we were looking at a collection of sketches of seagulls and sea lions.

"Really! That's wonderful," Joss said, glancing at me.

"Not really," I protested, holding up my hands and shaking my head.

"Yeah, you are," Sunil said, as my parents agreed.

"Dominic, you love to draw!" my mom said.

"Then you're an artist," Joss said, smiling.

I was blushing now and I didn't want to pursue

this topic of conversation. I only sketched as a hobby. I didn't have any plans to make it more than that.

"Well, we'd better get going," Dad said. "It was great to meet you both. Have a wonderful day."

He herded us back to the car.

I elbowed Sunil gently in the side. "Thanks a lot."

"You shouldn't deny your talent."

I blinked, taken aback by their statement and their faith in my abilities.

"You're passionate about your sketching, and you're really good. That's all I'm saying."

"Thanks."

None of my sketches were good enough for me. But at least other people liked them.

★★★

Mom and Dad took us to Lane's.

Sunil and I each ordered the cheeseburger and fries. I doused my fries in ketchup and stabbed them with my fork, shovelling a bunch into my mouth at once, while Sunil didn't put anything on theirs and picked them up one at a time in their fingers, eating with a grace I envied. I made sure I chewed with my mouth closed and wiped my chin with my napkin.

"So, Sunil, you're from Toronto?" my dad said.

"Yes." They glanced at me with some unease and I shrugged. I couldn't exactly stop my parents from asking questions.

"And you're here with your dad?" my mom asked.

"Yes."

"For the whole summer?" Mom asked.

"Most of it," Sunil said.

"What does your dad do for a living?" Dad chimed in.

"Dad. Come on. What's with the twenty questions?" I asked, embarrassed.

"I'm just making conversation. He doesn't have to tell us."

Sunil cleared his throat and said something but it wasn't audible.

"Pardon?" my mom said.

"I use the pronouns 'they/them,'" Sunil said,

   SUMMER WITH SUNIL

gazing at my parents with a steady confidence that impressed me.

"Oh, thank you for telling us," my mom said.

"Oh," my dad said, looking confused. "What did I say?"

"You said 'he,'" I explained.

Now Sunil looked uncomfortable, and I felt terrible. I needed to fix this situation, and fast. But my mom stepped in, as she usually did when my dad was floundering.

"Sunil, I'm glad that you and Dominic are striking up a friendship."

Sunil seemed relieved. "Thanks. Dominic's been so nice to me."

"I'm glad to hear it," my dad said, smiling through his confusion. "I'm sorry I used the wrong pronoun. Dominic explained to us how important it is to get it right."

I knew Dad didn't mean to cause any problems. It was hard for the old folks to understand the ways my generation had redefined genders and upended expectations. I got that, even though it was really frustrating sometimes.

We ate the rest of the meal and changed the topic to the weather and Joss Whitby's art. I was relieved when we were done.

"Thank you so much for lunch," Sunil said to my parents.

"Yeah, thanks. That was great," I said. "We're gonna take off, though. What time do you want to head back?"

"I don't know," my mom said. "Let's say three o'clock? So I'll have time to lie on the beach before supper."

Sightseeing with Sunil

LIVERPOOL WAS MUCH MORE INTERESTING with Sunil by my side.

"Where do you want to go first?" I asked.

"There's a cool park at the end of Main Street," Sunil said. "Sometimes you see things you'd never expect. I remember a very handsome, lost-looking guy who stared at me like he wanted to say hi but was way too shy."

I blushed. "I mean, we'd just gotten into town

and I was still pissed at my parents for dragging me away from my friends and the city. Probably wasn't the best time to say hi."

"Huh."

"But you were so . . . cute and, I don't know, you looked so cool. I wish I'd said something."

"Yeah?"

I nodded. "I looked for you everywhere, remember. Stalker level."

Sunil smiled as if that pleased them. A lot.

"I only came into town with my dad that one time. He spent the whole afternoon with his new woman. Gave me twenty bucks and told me to find something to do."

We'd been walking along the sidewalk over the bridge that went over the Mersey and into Liverpool and I stopped and stared at them.

"That's really shitty."

"Uh-huh. Why I opted to stay at the beach. I guess he figured that kept me out of the way, so he spent most of his time with her."

"I don't like to say it, but I think I hate your dad. And I've never met him."

Sunil gave me a wry smile. "Fair."

"Why do people have kids if they don't want to spend any time with them?"

Sunil shrugged. "I couldn't tell you. I probably won't have any."

"Me neither. Look, I'm sorry my parents were so curious at lunch."

"Eh, it was kind of nice to have them interested. Even if I was nervous."

"Hey, does your dad have a problem with . . ." I gestured vaguely at Sunil. ". . . the whole gender-queer thing?"

"He's not the most progressive-minded guy. Part of the reason my parents separated."

"Right."

"I make him uncomfortable. Toxic masculinity and all that. He doesn't get it."

"That's too bad."

"I can choose whether or not to visit him. I

thought this vacation was going to be something else, but now that I know this is how he's going to treat me, I'll think twice about visiting him again."

"I'm glad you came to Summerside Beach. I'm sorry he's not a good parent."

"I was considering telling my mom that I wanted to come home."

"You were?" I said.

"Yeah. But then I met this cute guy staying next door." They glanced at me and grinned.

I looked down at myself. "I'm cute? Really?"

"Not like a kid. I mean you're *cute* cute."

"You need to be more specific."

"Do I?" They smirked. "I think you get the picture."

I blushed and grinned. "Well, thanks."

"Also, friendly and smart and fun to hang out with."

"Geeze," I said, running a hand through my hair. I was embarrassed and didn't know what to say. But I was glad, too. "Thanks," I repeated. There was an awkward pause. "You're fun to hang out with, too."

 SUMMER WITH SUNIL

They smiled. "Huh. But not . . . cute?" They looked at the ground, then glanced up shyly.

"Sunil, you're freaking adorable. Shut up."

"Wow."

"And I wish I had half your style."

They threw their head back and twirled in place, their knee-length skirt flaring out.

★★★

The park was busier than I'd seen it yet.

"Have you been inside the lighthouse?" Sunil asked.

"Not yet."

I followed Sunil into the pyramid-shaped structure. The bottom floor of the lighthouse had become a gift shop.

"Hello," said a girl from behind the counter. "Welcome to the Fort Point Lighthouse."

She looked about our age. She grinned at us and snapped her gum.

"Hi," I said as Sunil smiled at her.

She looked at Sunil and gave them a once-over, then turned to me.

"Visiting Liverpool?"

"Yep. I'm from Ottawa, they're from Toronto."

Her eyes widened. "Ooh, city folk. How are you finding our boring old town?" She looked around as if her boss might show up. "I'm not really supposed to talk like that." She cleared her throat, straightened up and said, in a very fake way: "How are you enjoying the beautiful town of Liverpool, Nova Scotia, the Port of the Privateers?"

We stared at her and she broke up laughing. We couldn't help but join her.

"I mean, it's . . . small."

She sighed. "Yes, it is." She finger-gunned me. "But pretty."

I nodded and Sunil picked up a mason jar filled with purple liquid from its spot in a tub of ice.

"I'm getting some of this. It's what they serve at Lane's," they said to me.

Sunil turned the jar so I could see the label:

Blueberry Lemonade.

"That's the best! I drink gallons of it in the summer," the girl said. "My name's Tracy. And you are?" She seemed to be ignoring Sunil but was interested in me.

"I'm Dominic, and this is Sunil. We're staying at Summerside Beach."

When I told her my name, her smile lost some of its friendliness.

"Oh, I'm sorry. I thought you were a girl."

Sunil and I exchanged a glance.

I bristled. "No. By the way, do you sell postcards?"

"Yep. We've got some over there," she said, pointing to a spot in the corner and then returning to her stool behind the desk. She gave Sunil another assessing look and then ignored us.

Well, then. Screw you.

An elderly lady with a cane came into the gift shop, and Tracy turned, a glowing smile on her face. "Hi there. Welcome to Fort Point Park."

"You want one of these?" Sunil asked, pointing to the jars of blueberry lemonade.

"I don't know," I said, glancing at Tracy. "Not really in the mood anymore."

"Dominic. Don't let her ruin our afternoon. I'll get you one. On me," they said, scooping another lemonade out of the ice bucket and taking it to the cash.

Sunil gestured to a narrow stairway at the back of the lighthouse. "You can go up if you want, but it's not that high."

"Yeah, I'm good," I said.

Sunil took the lemonade to Tracy, who was looking everywhere but at us.

"Two of these, please."

Tracy turned to Sunil as if she'd just noticed them.

"Sure," she said, ringing up the drinks.

"You have really pretty eyes and a nice smile," they said, giving Tracy a smile of their own. It was a bold move.

Tracy blinked, opened her mouth, and then smiled, with an almost comical expression of surprise.

"Thanks. Enjoy the lemonade. If you don't mind bringing the jars back when you're done, we like to recycle them."

"Sure," Sunil said, pocketing their change and passing the second lemonade to me. "Thank you."

We found a spot by the railing, where I'd been when I first saw Sunil sitting on the bench. We drank our lemonade, watching the sailboats out on the ocean.

"That was a ballsy move," I said. "Well done."

They shrugged. "I like to give people the benefit of the doubt. Most of the time."

"Huh."

"We're lucky the weather's been so good," Sunil said, leaning on the railing, their jar of lemonade in one hand. Their chin-length, wavy hair blew in the salty breeze. "Lake Ontario is great, but it's not the ocean. Imagine how far this goes out."

I swallowed, trying to focus. "Yeah, I remember asking my mom one time when I was little, what was across the water, and she said England. That blew my mind. It still does."

Sunil nodded. "The smell of salt in the air. That's different from the lake."

"Do you like the city?"

Sunil glanced at me. "Huh. Most of the time. Sometimes it's too much. But I like to be where the people are." They grinned and I recognized the quote from *The Little Mermaid*.

"Yeah. I've been to Toronto, and it does seem huge compared to little old Ottawa. I'm definitely a city mouse. But I wish this place was closer, so it wasn't a big deal to visit once in a while."

11 # The Thrift Store

WE STOOD THERE sipping our blueberry lemonade for at least a half hour, maybe longer.

"You want to go shopping?" I said when we'd finished our drinks and Sunil had returned the empty mason jars to Tracy.

"Shopping?"

I nodded. "Yeah. I want to check out that thrift shop with the weird name. Guy's Frenchy's or something."

Sunil nodded. "Yeah, okay."

We walked back, talking about stupid stuff like our classes and what we hoped to study at university in a couple of years. Sunil had decided on doing an undergraduate degree in English and then maybe teachers college. They weren't sure where they wanted to study.

"You know, the University of Ottawa has a great Lit program," I said.

"You should do something with your art, Dominic. You're so talented."

"I don't know. It's just a hobby. I don't know if I want to study it."

"Sure. But maybe you could try digital design or something like that. That could be a cool career."

I groaned. "I don't want to think about having a career. I don't want to think about having to work for a living!"

In the thrift store, we were like little kids, finding all sorts of treasures and being silly. We tried on scarves and hats, teasing each other. Luckily there was hardly anyone else in there, which seemed weird. Then again, it was a weekday, so most people were at work.

Sunil had a bundle of things in their arms and so did I.

"I hope they have bags," they said.

"Yeah, me too. These prices are awesome."

"I'm glad we came."

On the drive back to Summerside, we told my parents about our haul at the thrift store and that they should check it out before we left.

Sunil and I hung out whenever we could.

When the weather was nice, we walked on the beach and laid on towels on the white sand, listening to the surf or to our music playlists, which we shared with each other. I made fun of Sunil's penchant for videogame soundtracks and they made fun of me for listening to Coldplay. But there were more similarities in our music tastes than differences. On rainy days, Sunil came over to my cottage and we hung out upstairs or in the living room if Mom and Dad had gone out.

One day, Sunil invited me over.

"My dad's still in Bridgewater — big surprise — so we have the cottage to ourselves. And he must have felt guilty because he loaded the fridge and the cupboards with really good stuff."

"I'm there," I said, ending the call. I threw on some jogging pants and grabbed a sweater — the breeze was chilly today and I didn't know if Sunil would have the heat on.

"I'm going next door," I said as I passed my parents, who were making breakfast.

"Good morning," my dad said, in a sarcastic way.

"Yeah, good morning."

"Oh, Dominic! Hold on a second," my mom said, cracking an egg on the side of a bowl. "We're going to get tickets to go whale watching at Digby Neck. Do you think Sunil might want to come?"

"Maybe. I'll ask them. I don't know if they have money to pay for a ticket . . ."

"Don't worry about that," my dad said. "We'll cover it."

"Cool, thanks."

My mom continued. "Just let me know soon because I want to book our tickets today. We want to get them for next Wednesday, so make sure Sunil doesn't already have plans with their dad."

No worries there.

"Sure, thanks. Later."

I made the short hop from our cottage to Sunil's. They'd told me they'd leave the front door unlocked and to just come in. I opened it and called out, "Honey, I'm home," just to be cheeky.

Sunil was in the kitchen.

"Cute. Honey, I'm just making coffee."

"Oh, cool. Is there enough for me?"

"There will be. Have I won you over?"

"Too soon to tell. I just like when you make it for me."

"Aw," they said, blushing and smiling. "Flatterer."

"So, what kind of stuff did your dad bring us?"

"Have a look," they said, motioning to the cupboard.

I walked over and opened one.

"Oh, hell yes. What a king!" Then I glanced at Sunil. "Oh, sorry. King of the stealth supply run?"

They laughed. "I guess so. Nice save."

"Thanks. I'll be here all week."

My gaze roamed over the bags of chips and popcorn and pretzels, and packages of sweet treats and candy.

"Holy shit. That's quite the haul."

"That's how he makes up for abandoning me."

"Hell . . . it would be nice if your dad wanted to actually spend time with you but . . . can I just say, screw him? Let's party!"

Sunil raised one of the empty coffee mugs. "But first coffee and you need to eat something healthy if you're gonna binge on this crap all day."

"Sure, sure. I'll have one of these granola bars."

They levelled a gaze at me that reminded me of some of the looks my mom gave me.

"I'm making us scrambled eggs."

I laughed. "Fine."

I sat on a stool at the breakfast bar while Sunil cooked. It was weirdly domestic but I liked it. They seemed to know how to handle themselves around a stove and I admired that. I was only just learning the basics now and resisting it.

"Are you adding Tabasco?"

They peeked around at me. "Just a little. It gives it a lift."

"Hmm. I'm going to reserve judgement on that," I said, frowning.

"Oh, come on, Dominic. Live a little."

Well, it turned out that a bit of Tabasco sauce mixed in with scrambled eggs was freaking incredible.

"Wait, these are literally the best," I said, my mouth stuffed full of the delicious creation. "Why have I never had this?"

Sunil shrugged, eating much more daintily than me, as I shovelled eggs into my gob. They watched me with the focus of a zoologist observing an animal in the wild.

"Sorry," I mumbled. "I'm just hungry."

Sunil laughed. "Huh. It's nice to see someone go after what they want with so much . . . passion."

We stared at each other as I chewed and I wondered if they were actually thinking about me eating these eggs or . . . something else.

12 *The Game*

AFTER WE HAD BREAKFAST, we hung out in the living room and I watched Sunil play *The Last of Us*.

"My dad wouldn't let me bring my actual gaming system," I said. "I have my handheld but that's it."

Sunil glanced at me. I realized after I'd said it that it might have been a bit insensitive, as Sunil's dad obviously didn't care what they did to pass the time.

"Anyway, this is a cool game. I've heard of it but never played it," I added.

"My favourite. I've played through it about ten times already."

"You're really good!" I meant that. The way they were blasting through encounters with infected and hunters, getting all the things they needed to progress the story, it was pretty humbling. "The graphics are amazing."

"Yeah. I like games like this with a story and great visuals. Plus, a killer soundtrack. It's almost like being in a movie."

"Oh shit, I almost forgot. My parents want to know if you want to come whale watching with us next week."

"Really?"

"Yeah. You don't have to, but if you want to, it would be cool. Do you even like whales?"

"I like whales."

"Want to come?"

"Sure. Let me know how much the ticket is and I'll email you the money."

"No, no, my parents are paying. It's a sweet deal."

"I've got money. Again, a guilty dad is not an entirely bad thing."

"Sunil. They said they'd cover it. It's not worth it to argue."

Sunil laughed. "Fine."

I texted my mom that Sunil was in. I felt good about offering them some family time, even if it wasn't with their family. We could be their surrogate family. Except then I might feel like we were siblings or something, which I really didn't want to feel, considering some of the *other* feelings I was having for Sunil.

"Have you ever made out with anyone?" I said. It just came out. Sometimes I had no filter.

Sunil's head swivelled toward me and then back to their game, where they ended up dying by zombie attack.

"Shit! Dammit," they muttered.

"Sorry. I distracted you."

Sunil paused the game and gave me their full attention.

"Did you seriously just ask me if I'd ever made

out with anyone? While I was being attacked by a clicker?"

"A what?"

"It's a kind of . . . zombie. Except the people aren't actually dead. They've been taken over by a fungus."

"There are different kinds of fungus zombies?"

Sunil shook their head but I was glad to see a wry smile. "So, did you really ask me that?"

"Uh. Yeah." *No going back now, I guess.*

"Wow. That's epic level awkward" they said.

"So, have you?" I pressed. For some reason, I needed to know.

"Not really."

I narrowed my eyes. "What does that mean?"

They shrugged and put the controller down. "It means that I started to once and didn't like it much. So, I stopped."

"Oh." I thought about that. "Does that mean you're . . . asexual?"

Sunil gave me a look. "Huh? I don't know. Maybe.

Or maybe I just didn't like making out with her."

"Oh. Right. Sorry."

"It's okay. I don't have all the answers yet, you know." They smiled at me and I felt better. Sunil took a deep breath. "If you're asking if I ever have sex on the brain, then yeah, I do. I have feelings like that. I don't think I'm asexual."

"Okay. Well, do you want to date hes or shes or theys? Or do you know yet?"

"I don't really care. I'm attracted to the person. Not the gender."

"Me too. Is that pansexual? I've always thought of myself as bisexual," I said.

Sunil turned the controller off and set it down.

"Dominic. I feel like this conversation is getting way serious. Why does the word matter, if you know who you're attracted to, and who you are?"

I nodded. "Sure. I guess."

"Or even if you don't. We need to normalize not having everything figured out. Not defining every little thing about ourselves. We're not dictionaries.

We're people. We're just trying to live our lives in the face of a global extinction event."

I blinked. "Wow. That's powerful."

"I'll put it on a T-shirt," they said, grinning and going back to their game. "Don't get me wrong, I know that labels are hugely important for a lot of people. But for me, I don't feel like I need to define every aspect of myself so that other people can 'get' me. Most people either get me or don't when they meet me, and I'm not interested in forcing them." They looked into my eyes with some emotion. "I know *you* get me. I knew it from the start."

13 The Dog

SUNIL'S WORDS MADE ME THINK and I had a strong urge to lean over and try to kiss them. But that would mean asking if that was okay. And I wasn't brave enough yet.

"Do you want to go for a walk?" I blurted.

"Sure," they said, saving the game and putting down their controller. "I'm too distracted to play."

"Oh, shit. Sorry for all the talking."

They looked at me, with something other than

frustration in their eyes. "It wasn't the talking."

Oh! Did they mean they were having kissing thoughts about me? I blushed and panicked. And stood up.

Then Sunil stood too. "Okay, let's go."

The long stretch of Summerside Beach felt safe and familiar. I took Sunil's hand when they offered it.

We spoke about the ocean and the seagulls and the jellyfish and the shells that lay half-buried in the wet sand. Every time Sunil found a sand dollar, they made a little sound of pleasure and dug it out, holding it in their palm like it was solid gold. They'd painted their short fingernails a vibrant blue.

"You like those," I said.

"I used to collect them when I was little. I started to again this summer. But when they dry up, they tend to crack and break, and you're left with a pile of shards."

They put it down gently on top of the sand and tossed the hair out of their eyes.

"You ever feel like that, Dominic?"

"Huh? Like what?"

Sunil shrugged, looked out to sea, then back at me. "Like so delicate that a strong wind might break you?"

"Sometimes."

Sunil laughed. "I get emotional over stupid stuff. Sorry."

I tugged them closer. "That's not stupid."

"Okay."

"Better to get emotional over stuff like that than never feel anything."

"Are you speaking from experience?"

"Yeah, well, I think every one of us has seen too much awful crap, you know? The internet is great in some ways, but it's honestly horrible in lots of others. I've seen things . . ."

Sunil squeezed my hand. "I know. Me too. And by the time you realize you probably shouldn't have watched or looked, it's too late."

"Yeah."

We heard barking and looked up as a tornado of white and brown fur came toward us. Sunil shrank back and pulled their hand free.

It was pure instinct that made me move in front of them and wave my arms at the animal.

"Hey! Back off," I said. I wasn't afraid of dogs and I didn't think this one was about to attack. Sure enough, as soon as I made a show of confidence, the dog backed up and sat down.

I looked around for its owner.

A blonde-haired woman ran toward us.

"Can you get your dog, please?" I asked, my voice betraying my frustration. I realized that people liked to let their dogs off leash at the beach, but honestly, it might be better to do it when it wasn't so crowded.

"I'm so sorry. He's friendly!" she said. "Halo! Leave those boys alone."

The dog looked at Sunil and then at me, then ran toward its owner. I glanced quickly at Sunil, aware that they might feel hurt at being misgendered, while my own queer joy lifted at being seen for who I was. But Sunil was still staring at the dog and hugging their arms.

"I think it just wanted to make friends," I said, glancing at Sunil, who still looked scared. "Are you okay?"

"Can we go back?"

"But we just came out."

We'd only gone half the distance we usually did on our beach walks.

Sunil gazed in the direction the dog and its owner had gone. Halo bounced along beside the woman now, acting as if he hadn't just made my friend lose their shit.

"Sunil, I'm not gonna let you get hurt. It's just a dog."

Maybe it was the wrong thing to say. I knew that because Sunil frowned and shook their head. They turned and started walking back toward the cottages.

Shit, shit, shit. Way to go, Dominic.

I caught up to them.

"Hey, I'm sorry."

They glanced at me but didn't reply.

"Are you mad about being mistaken for a guy?"

"No. Happens sometimes." Their words were short and abrupt.

"You don't like dogs," I stated.

"No."

Well. This was the first thing we'd discovered where we were at odds, because I loved dogs. We didn't have one, only because my mom didn't want to deal with the mess. But I had big plans for my life. I wanted *all the dogs.*

But I also wanted to be friends with Sunil. And that was the most time-sensitive thing at the moment.

"Yeah, I don't know why people let their dogs off-leash. I'm sure I've seen Leash Your Dog signs."

Sunil was quiet and walking along with a grim expression. They didn't reply and I wondered if I'd just screwed everything up. But all I'd done was protect them and then . . . oh damn.

"Hey, I'm sorry," I said again. "I didn't realize how scared you were."

Sunil stopped walking and turned toward me. I'd never seen them look so upset. "I hate being scared. I know it was 'just a dog.' I wish I wasn't terrified of a family pet."

I remembered thinking this delicate, feminine person could be fierce in the right circumstances. I'd been right.

"I'm sorry." I didn't know what else I was supposed to say. I felt awful.

We stood staring at each other for a long moment.

"You know I'd have beat it with a piece of driftwood or something if it had tried to attack you, right?" I said.

Sunil stared at me, various emotions playing on their face. The corner of their lip twitched.

I stepped forward carefully. "You're safe with me. I promise."

They looked down at the sand and kicked it with the toe of their boot. "I'm not a maiden in distress, you know."

"I wouldn't care if you were."

They rolled their eyes and smiled. "I don't hate *all* dogs."

"I know." I mean, I didn't, but I was glad to hear it.

"It just . . . took me by surprise. And I didn't know what it was gonna do."

I nodded. "Fair. Did you . . . have you been attacked by a dog before?"

They nodded. "Yeah, when I was five. Got bit, too. On my ankle. I can show you the scar."

"I believe you. And, shit, no wonder you were scared."

They gazed down the beach again, in the direction we'd been walking. "If you want, I guess we can keep going."

"Nah. Looks like it might rain. Let's go pig out on junk."

14 The Whales

WE HUNG OUT AT SUNIL'S COTTAGE, eating chips and cheese puffs and M&Ms all afternoon, and watching movies on Netflix.

Mom texted me to ask if I was coming back to our cottage for supper.

"My mom wants to know about dinner. But I'm so full I don't think I could even eat."

"You can stay here."

"Okay." I texted her that I was staying at

Sunil's for supper but I'd be back at our cottage by nine or ten.

We didn't actually get hungry again until around seven, when Sunil brought out a pre-made pasta salad from the fridge and popped several frozen hash browns in the toaster oven. We ate them at the breakfast bar in comfortable silence and talked about the movies we'd watched.

"I guess I'd better head back," I said finally.

"Sure. Thanks for coming over," they said, as they walked me the short distance to the door. "Um, my dad is actually gonna be here tomorrow so maybe we can get together the day after?"

"Oh," I said. "Sure. Keep me posted."

"Bye, Dominic. Don't let the bed bugs bite."

I laughed and then sobered. "Wait, do you think there might be bed bugs here?"

"Oh my god, Dominic. Good night."

"Good night," I said, heading in and thinking about little, tiny bugs in my bed.

I knew it was just an expression. But I also knew

that bed bugs had become a problem in lots of places. And I hadn't really thought about that before today.

When I pulled back the bedclothes that night, I examined the sheets for dots of blood or any little black bugs. Then, taking a deep breath, I checked in the corners of the bed frame and under the mattress. Luckily, there were no obvious signs of the little critters. I dropped the mattress back and it made a loud *thwunk*.

"What are you doing up there?" my dad yelled.

"Looking for bed bugs," I called back. "Didn't see any."

"Thank god. Wait, does Sunil's cottage have them?"

"No, no. It's fine. Never mind." I didn't want to explain how a simple good night had turned into this. "Good night!"

"Good night, Dominic. Don't let the bed bugs bite," my dad said, with a certain smugness, and I heard my mom giggle.

Man. So hilarious, those two.

★★★

When the day of the whale-watching trip came, Sunil met us on our front porch.

"Thanks again for bringing me, Mr. and Mrs. Dunn."

"Oh, Sunil, it's not a problem at all. It's nice for Dominic to have a friend along. We're just the boring old parents," my mom said.

"Oh, you're not that old," I said, not mentioning the boring part.

"Very funny," my dad said, ruffling my hair as he passed.

"Oh, my god, Dad, I'm not eight years old," I said, frantically fixing the style that I'd spent time arranging that morning. Sunil laughed softly.

They mouthed "You're cute," to me and I gave them the finger behind my parents' backs.

The drive to Digby took about an hour. It was straight across the Nova Scotia peninsula, from the south side to the north side. The road went through a nature reserve so there wasn't much except for trees and bush, but it was a peaceful drive. Sunil and I had our earbuds in and my parents listened to the radio. I had the urge to hold Sunil's hand, since we did that a lot, but it took me ages to get up the nerve. Finally, I closed my eyes for a second, took a deep breath and reached out, covering the top of Sunil's hand gently with mine. They turned their hand over and laced our fingers together. I went back to looking out the window, proud of myself for being brave enough to make a move, and thrilled that Sunil had responded. I think I had a smile on my face for the entire rest of the journey.

The whale-watching company did their business out of Digby Neck, which looked like it would be another half hour along the coast from Digby itself. We stopped for a quick lunch off the highway, just outside of town. Dad said we'd come back to Digby for supper, but that we needed to get to Petit Passage in time to check in and board the boat.

The drive was really beautiful, with glimpses of the Bay of Fundy. We got to the place with lots of time to spare. Petit Passage was a spot on the bar where the land split and the ocean came through a narrow channel. The whale-watching tour company was called Petit Passage Whale Watch, and it came highly rated. It was a family-run business, with one boat, and my parents had decided it was our best bet for a good chance to see some whales.

We handed in our tickets at the white clapboard building perched on the rocks, with Whale's Tail Cafe in pretty blue lettering and a picture of a whale's tail lifting from the water. Sunil bought some cookies and shared them with me.

"Is there a bathroom on the boat?" my mom asked my dad.

"I think so."

"I'm going to check," she said, looking worried.

I grinned at Sunil. "Bladder issues," I said.

My dad frowned at me.

"What? It's true," I said.

"I don't know if she wants you telling all your friends, Dominic."

"One friend. I told one friend," I said.

Dad smiled at Sunil. "Yes, well, Sunil's getting all the family secrets now."

"Bladder incontinence? Some secret." I laughed.

"Dominic."

"I'm sorry. I'll shut up. I'm just excited about seeing the whales."

"Be nice if there's a bathroom on board," Sunil said, "Just in case."

"Yes, I agree," my dad said. "Who knows how long we'll be out there."

My mom came back, beaming from ear-to-ear. "There is a bathroom. The woman I spoke to said that the whales are pretty far out today, so we're in for a ride."

The Petit Passage Whale Watching boat was a respectable size, I was glad to see. There were probably about fifty people and it wasn't too crowded. There were seats all along the outside of the deck and two rows of seats down the middle.

The kid organizing the passengers, who didn't

look much older than me and Sunil, used a wired intercom to introduce himself as Dustin, and repeated what my mom said about the whales being far out in the bay, so we should prepare for a decent journey. He said it might take an hour or more to get to them.

There was hardly any wind and the sky was free of clouds. The forecast was for a clear and mild day. We'd brought jackets for warmth as it had said on the website that it was chilly out on the ocean.

"I have Gravol in my purse if anyone starts feeling sick," Mom said. She and my dad had found a spot on the middle bench seat, and Sunil and I sat opposite them by the rail.

"Well, it's a gorgeous day for a sea voyage," Dad said, putting an arm around her and kissing the top of her head.

I glanced at Sunil who gazed wistfully at them for a second, then turned their gaze to the horizon. We watched the land get smaller and smaller as we headed out to sea.

Dustin explained that the whales were always in a

different spot each day, but that he and his family knew where to look. He talked about the other seabirds and marine animals that made use of the area and said we should keep our eyes out for seals and puffins.

After about thirty or forty minutes, the land became a tiny strip of gray in the far distance. Another ten or fifteen and we felt like we were in the middle of the ocean. It was stunning and peaceful and utterly beautiful.

"Okay. I can see a couple of other Whale Watchers up ahead so we must be getting close," Dustin said. He lifted his binoculars again. "Oh yeah, there we go! If you look out to your starboard side you might see some whales breaching in the distance. That's the right side, for you landlubbers. We're still far away. As we get closer, things should get much more interesting!"

We craned our heads to see past the cabin. The boats in the distance were small specks on the surface of the sea.

"I want to remind everyone that those on the outside

bench can kneel on it, and the people in the middle seats can stand on them if they like, but please be careful. Sue-Ann and Brady can help if you need anything, and they're going to keep an eye on things on deck."

We looked up at the two crew members with the Petit Passage ball caps who had moved to stand near the stern and waved at us with friendly smiles.

"That would be a cool job," I said.

"Yeah," they agreed.

Sunil's gaze was focused on the ocean in the direction that Dustin had said the whales would be. Their eyes were wide and bright, and they were flushed with excitement. The wind blew their hair back from their face and I didn't think I'd ever seen them look so beautiful. I was entranced, and for a moment, I forgot about the whales.

Then they noticed I was staring.

"What?"

I averted my eyes and said, "Nothing." I kept glancing back at them. It was hard to turn away.

"Dominic. What are you doing? You know there are whales over there . . ."

"I know."

Dustin's voice came on the announcer again.

"Okay, we're getting close now! Look out to starboard. There's a pod of about six or seven Humpbacks putting on a show!"

Sunil and I stood up like we were one person and moved to the middle of the boat.

"Come on!" they said, getting up onto the seat and urging me to do the same. My parents had gone around to the edge on the starboard side.

"Oh, holy shit!" I said, "There's one!"

"Oh wow!" Sunil said. The dark shadow of a huge Humpback whale slid under the surface, about twenty metres away, its broad back breaking the water.

"There's another one!" someone shouted. Now everyone's attention was focused on the water, and whales were swimming close enough to see clearly, their small dorsal fins and grey backs surfacing. In the distance, a Humpback's front half came right out of the water before splashing down again.

I forgot about everything else.

My dad had his camera with its giant zoom lens attached as he snapped photos. My mom looked flushed and excited as she watched. I'd never been up close to anything like a humpback whale before, and the experience was like nothing else.

"Do you think one will jump?" Sunil asked, bringing me back to the moment.

"I hope so," I said.

I caught movement to my right and turned my head just in time to see a whale stick its big mouth and head out of the water.

"Shit, look!" I grabbed Sunil's elbow and tugged them so they gazed in the same direction.

"Oh wow!" They laughed. "That thing could swallow me whole!"

As we watched that whale, behind it another one vaulted up out of the water with the grace of a winged creature and then came down on its side with a huge splash. Everyone in the boat cheered.

"Holy shit, holy shit, holy shit!" I exclaimed.

"That was so damn cool," Sunil said, meeting my gaze.

"Yeah. Cool," I said, caught up in their beauty again.

Sunil was just as unique and captivating as the creatures swimming around us.

15 Dinner in Digby

WE WATCHED THE POD of humpback whales frolic and play for about thirty or forty minutes, and then Dustin said we had to start back so we'd get back to Petit Passage in time for supper. He thanked everyone and let us know the return trip would take about an hour and a half, and that they had warm blankets for anyone who might be feeling chilled.

"I think we picked the right whale-watching service," my dad said and I had to agree. The trip had been a huge success and a fantastic way to spend an afternoon.

We found spots on the rail again while my parents cozied up in the middle seats under a wool blanket.

"Well, now we can say we've been close to a humpback whale," I said to Sunil.

"Yep. That was one of the most incredible experiences of my life. I need to thank your parents."

"They could tell you were having a good time."

"If you and your parents didn't come to Summerside Beach . . ." Sunil looked like they were about to cry.

"You wanna rest your head on my shoulder?" I asked.

Sunil moved closer, then scanned the people nearby.

"I don't think anyone will care. For all they know, we could be related — cousins or siblings," I whispered.

"Sure," Sunil said. "Okay."

I turned around to face my parents and shoved my hands into the pockets of my jacket, pulling my ball cap down a bit. Sunil leaned against me and rested their head on my shoulder.

The rocking of the boat made a pleasant rhythm. My mom's gaze met mine and she smiled. I returned it, then closed my eyes and leaned my head against Sunil's.

★★★

By the time we docked at Petit Passage, it was almost five-thirty.

"Sorry we got back so late," Dustin said over the announcements. "But I hope you'll all agree that it was worth the journey!"

There were cheers and agreements as people got organized to get off the boat. We stepped from the vessel with the rest of the group and made our way up the shore to the parked car.

"That was unbelievable," Sunil said. "Thank you so much for bringing me."

"We're glad to have you, Sunil," my mom said.

"Not a problem," my dad said.

I could tell they were impressed with Sunil's

politeness and their quiet intelligence. My parents were not always pleased with the friends I brought home, but how could they resist Sunil?

The drive back to Digby took about thirty minutes. My mom had looked up restaurants so it didn't take long to find a table at the Portside View. Huge square windows looked out on Digby Harbour, so that anywhere you were seated, you had an incredible view of the waterfront.

"Did you get some good shots of the whales, Dad?"

I'd taken a few with my phone but then had decided to be in the moment with Sunil and let my dad memorialize the occasion with his fancy camera and pricey zoom lens.

"Yeah, I think so. We can have a look through them when we get back." He nodded to Sunil. "Sunil, do you need to let your dad know we're a bit later than we planned? We probably won't get back to Summerside Beach until nine."

Sunil smiled. "I'll text him."

We glanced at each other as we ate, knowing

there was no need but I was glad Sunil had given the impression of being in touch with their dad. Not for the first time, I wondered if I should tell my parents that Sunil was alone at the resort. But what could they do about it? Sunil was seventeen and could legally live on their own in Ontario if they wanted to. But maybe in the name of honesty and full disclosure, I should let my parents know. Not right now, while Sunil was here. Maybe I'd tell them after we got home. I felt bad keeping it from them when they were being so thoughtful about including Sunil in our outings.

Sunil ordered the fish and chips, and I had lobster macaroni and cheese, and we shared. I tried not to notice the attentive expressions on my parents' faces. I think they were starting to see that Sunil and I were a little closer than regular friends. But maybe I was just paranoid, and anyway, I didn't care.

My mom fell asleep in the car on the way home. She did pretty well managing her disease, but the fatigue was something that she struggled with. She usually had a nap when she got home from work during the school year — it was the only way she could manage working full time. She and my dad were considering her going part-time so that she didn't get so tired out. There were instances when she'd needed a cane for balance for a few weeks, but her body had always recovered fully from those relapses so far.

Sunil and I tried not to laugh when she started to snore. My dad cranked the music. Mom could sleep through just about anything.

By the time we got back to the beach cottages, it was almost nine-thirty and getting pretty dark, the familiar sound of the surf crashing onto the rocks and sand was a cheery welcome.

Sunil thanked my parents and me, and keyed themselves into their cottage. I saw my mom staring at the cottage with narrowed eyes. Sunil hadn't left any lights on and I bet she was wondering where their father was.

16 *The Truth*

"DOMINIC . . . Sunil isn't there all by themselves, are they?" Mom asked.

I shook my head. "Um, not officially."

"What does that mean?" Dad asked, unpacking his fancy camera.

I kicked off my shoes and hung up my jacket.

"Okay, so, their dad isn't staying there exactly. But he's nearby," I explained.

"Nearby?" My mom's concerned expression

vanished. "Oh! They could afford to rent a cottage just for Sunil? And Sunil's dad is staying somewhere else in the resort?"

"Not exactly." I sat on the sofa.

"Dominic, what's going on?" my dad said, in his 'you'd better tell me this instant' voice.

I sighed. "Sunil's dad is staying in Bridgewater with his," I made air quotes, "ladyfriend."

"Not Sunil's mom, I take it?" Dad said.

"Oh," Mom said. "Wow. That's some A-plus parenting right there."

"I know, right?"

"And Sunil's . . . okay with that?" Dad asked, sitting at the table and scrolling through the shots he'd taken on his camera.

"I mean, they're making the best of it," I said. "They were gonna go back home to Toronto early but . . . uh, changed their mind when I showed up."

"Uh-huh."

"Hmm. So, when you've gone over there, it's just been the two of you?" my mom asked, trying to sound casual.

"Do you have a problem with that?" I tried not to sound pissed off at the question but I guess I failed.

"Don't use that tone with your mother, Dominic."

"I don't really have a *problem* with it," Mom said. "You're sixteen, almost seventeen. You're responsible. I only wish I'd known."

"Why exactly?"

She shrugged. "I don't know. Maybe I could have checked in on Sunil now and then."

"It's fine. I've been keeping close tabs."

"We noticed," Dad said.

"Their dad comes by occasionally. He stocks the fridge and the cupboards."

"Then leaves?"

"Yeah."

"Wow. That's . . . not ideal," Dad said mildly.

I laughed. "Jeez, Dad, try to control your outrage."

"Very funny," Dad said, putting his camera down. "It's not right. I don't care if Sunil's seventeen. Even if he was nineteen, I'd think it was pretty shitty."

"They."

"Pardon?"

"Even if *they* were nineteen."

"Yes. I'm sorry. *They.*"

My mom came over and put her hand on my shoulder. "Honey, are you and Sunil . . . together?"

"Doreen," my dad said, in a warning tone.

"What? I'm just asking."

"What makes you think they're more than friends?" my dad asked, giving me a glance. "I'm sure Sunil and Dominic are just friends. Right?"

Hmm. Now I had a choice to make.

"Actually, we're a little more than friends."

Both my parents turned to me, their eyes wide.

"Really," my dad said, his voice dull. He didn't sound too excited about it.

"Well, I think Sunil's adorable and you could do a lot worse," my mom said, with a cheeky smile.

"Uh, thanks? What the hell?"

"I don't know what to say!" she laughed. "Congratulations?"

I shook my head, making for the stairs. "Oh my god. You guys just . . ."

"Oh, come on, give us a break, Dominic. We're trying," Dad said.

I turned to face them. "Look, we're into each other. In a way that's more than just friends. That's all you need to know. All right?"

They exchanged a look and then my mom nodded. "Sure."

My dad didn't say anything.

I started to head upstairs.

"Dominic," my dad said.

I stared at the step I'd put my foot on.

"Just . . . be smart, all right? And, you know . . . careful."

I was glad I was facing away from them because my cheeks were burning and I had to blink the emotion back. He meant to be careful because even though I was a guy in my head, my body was capable of things that might prove . . . inconvenient. Again, the dysphoria slammed me in the face.

"Thanks," I said, and escaped.

I shut the door and texted Sunil.

Dom: Can I call you?

I got a response back almost instantly.

Sunil: Sure . . .

I hit the button to call and they picked up right away.

"Hi, Dominic."

"Hey. Listen, my parents were asking questions. I had to tell them."

"Tell them what?"

I groaned. "Well, kind of everything. About your dad. About . . . us."

"What was their reaction?"

"They weren't too impressed with your dad."

Sunil laughed softly. "That's fair. I'm not either."

"I, uh . . . they asked if we were more than friends . . ."

There was silence. All I could hear was Sunil's breathing.

"What did you say?"

"Yes. I said 'yes.' Aren't we?"

"I think so," Sunil said. "Yeah."

"I want to ask you . . ." I swallowed. I didn't think this would be so hard. "If you want to be my . . . my partner? That sounds so formal. I'm trying not to be gender specific here . . ."

I heard the smile in Sunil's voice when they answered. "You could take a page from the fifties and ask me if I want to go steady."

I laughed nervously. "Do you?"

"With you, Dominic? Definitely."

I couldn't help the grin that formed on my blushing face. "The only thing, though, is that . . . you're gonna go back to Toronto at the end of the summer, and I'm gonna go back to Ottawa."

"So?"

"So . . . how is that gonna work?"

"Let's worry about that later."

"Fine."

"Good."

"Good."

"And Dominic? Your parents are great."

"Yeah, I guess." I hated to admit it.

"You're lucky."

"Huh?"

"They care enough to ask important questions."

"Yeah, the only problem is, now they know we're alone when we're at your place."

"Huh. Do you think they're going to let you come over again?"

"Yeah. Of course. It's 2023. I'm on the goddamned pill."

"Dominic! Oh my god." They snorted and choked.

I laughed so hard I fell off the bed.

The Bonfire

MY PARENTS WERE PRETTY GOOD, even though they knew the truth about Sunil and me. They watched us a bit more closely, but they didn't get in the way of us being together. I was almost seventeen, after all.

Sunil and I spent our days in each other's company, walking the beach or exploring the nearby landscape. A few days after the whale-watching trip, we spent the afternoon at Sunil's place again, eating junk food and playing video games and streaming movies. It was getting late and I was thinking about heading back to my cottage.

"Hey, someone's having a party on the beach," Sunil said. They were looking out the front window. I walked over and peered outside.

Summerside Beach curved away from the cottages in a wide arc that came back around, so we could see most of the beach. About halfway down, orange flames danced against the night sky and illuminated a group of people who seemed to be having a good time.

"Let's go see," I said, eager for a closer look.

"Okay," Sunil said. "Let me just get my sweater."

I popped my head next door. "We're just going for a walk on the beach. I've got my phone."

"Sure," my dad said.

"Have fun," Mom added.

They were in the middle of a game of Scrabble, so they didn't pay much attention.

Sunil let me borrow a sweatshirt, which I pulled over my T-shirt, glad I was wearing rolled-up jeans instead of shorts. It had gotten chilly.

"Let's go," I said. I took Sunil's hand and we walked along, confident that no-one could see us very well in the darkness.

As we approached the bonfire, the sounds of people laughing and yelling could be heard over the pop of wood and the roar of flames. It wasn't until we got close that we could tell it was a group of kids our age, most of them holding bottles and drinking as they watched the bonfire.

Sunil and I stood at the edge of the water and watched. It was dark enough that we thought nobody would notice. But then someone from the party came toward us and Sunil let go of my hand and stepped back.

It was a guy in a football jersey smoking a cigarette. He looked us over. "Tourists I take it? Staying at the resort?"

Neither of us said anything.

The guy laughed and turned to another kid who had come up behind him. "Look at this guy in a frilly skirt," the first boy said, sneering at Sunil. "I guess this is how they dress in the big city."

"You don't even know where I'm from," Sunil said.

"Oh, I'm sorry. Are you from around here?"

"Come on, Dominic," Sunil said. "Let's go."

The guy's eyes widened. "Dominic? That's a cool name for a . . ." He looked me up and down and I stood taller and planted my boots in the sand, my legs apart.

"A what? What were you going to say?" I was so mad. I didn't even care that I might get my head beat in. How dare this kid deliberately bait us. We might not be locals but we had a right to be on the beach.

Someone else came up behind the two guys.

"Lars. Leave these kids alone. Stop being a dick."

Lars laughed and threw his cigarette in the sand, then he and the other guy turned and walked off toward the bonfire.

My heart was beating rapidly and the anger was still swimming in my head.

The girl who had chased the guys away looked us over and smiled. "We're not all small-town assholes," she said. "I'm Laura."

Relief pushed some of the anger away, but I was still wary. I didn't smile but I shook Laura's outstretched hand.

"Dominic. This is Sunil."

"I'm sorry about Lars and Mike. They're idiots. Come have a drink with us. There's lots of beer and I think a couple of bottles of wine going around."

Sunil and I exchanged a glance. She seemed genuine and harmless but I wasn't sure about the rest of them.

"Thanks, but we'd better get back," I said, as Sunil nodded in agreement.

A shout broke the peaceful evening.

"Sunil!"

Sunil looked up as a middle-aged man in jeans and a windbreaker hastened along the beach toward us.

"Oh no," they said. "Shit."

"Is that . . ."

"Yes." Sunil looked upset as they walked toward the man who had called their name.

I didn't know what to do, but I stayed where I was as Sunil had an animated conversation with their dad several feet away. I couldn't hear what was said, but I could tell they were both angry and not really hiding it.

Laura drifted back to the bonfire after a last look at us.

After a few minutes, Sunil came over to me. "Sorry, but I have to go."

I watched as they followed their dad along the beach, toward the cottages. When I got myself together, I jogged to catch up to them. Sunil was keeping a distance from their father so if I kept my voice low, maybe he wouldn't notice.

"Hey," I said to Sunil. "What's going on?"

"My dad was expecting me to be at the resort. Apparently, he doesn't want me to go anywhere or do anything while I'm holed up here."

"What?" Literally the only thing that made their dad's neglect tolerable was the freedom they'd had. "That's bullshit."

Sunil's dad was suddenly in front of me, his hands on his hips as he looked me over. "Who the hell are you?"

"I'm Dominic. I'm Sunil's friend." This probably wasn't the time to declare our romantic attachment. I put my hand out for a shake but he ignored it.

"Sunil doesn't need any friends. He has lots back home."

"How the hell do you know?" Sunil said, shaking their head. "And it's 'they.' I've told you."

"Don't talk to me like that. And this isn't the time to worry about pronouns."

"Really, Dad? So, when is the time to worry about my feelings and what I want?"

"Sunil, you're seventeen. You don't know what you want."

Sunil stood there and crossed their arms over their chest. "I'm not a child."

"Yes, you are. Come on."

"If I'm a child, then why am I living at this cottage all by myself? Why aren't you staying with me?"

Sunil's dad frowned. "Do you know how much money I've spent on you, Sunil? That fancy beach cottage cost more than you'd believe. And I bring you all those groceries. I'm looking after you, but I don't think I need to hold your hand all the time. I do expect you not to go out gallivanting late at night and hanging out at bonfires with older teenagers."

We were close to the cottages now, thank god. I kind of wanted to just go past Sunil's dad to get to mine, but I didn't want to go near him either. And I needed to give Sunil my support, anyway. Even if his dad scared me.

Sunil's dad was white, like me, and only slightly taller than Sunil.

"Now you care what I'm doing?" Sunil asked with bitterness.

"What are you talking about?"

Sunil spread their arms. "You only brought me here so you could get away with your girlfriend. You've hardly spent any time with me!"

Sunil's dad didn't say anything. He glanced at me, then looked at Sunil.

"That's enough, Sunil."

Sunil pushed past me and their dad, and ran toward the cottages.

Their dad looked at me. "Where are your parents . . . Dominic?" He said my name like it hurt him to do so.

I tried to keep my voice steady even though the anger that had ebbed and flowed all night was hovering right below the surface now.

"They're in the cottage beside yours."

He processed this. "Do they know you're out wandering in the dark with my son?"

I spoke through clenched teeth and held Sunil's dad's gaze. "They know exactly where I am and who I'm with. Because we're staying on this beach together. As a family."

Sunil's dad stared at me. He looked me up and down, opened his mouth, then closed it. He shook his head as if I wasn't even worth the trouble, then walked off after Sunil.

I let out a shaky breath and stood there for several minutes, clenching and unclenching my hands and

　　　　SUMMER WITH SUNIL

trying to get my breathing back to normal. Eventually, I made it back.

My dad glanced up from the Scrabble board when I came in. "How was your walk?"

"Eventful," I said.

They both looked over at me.

"Are you okay?" my mom said, starting to stand.

I gestured behind me. "Sunil's dad just showed up, out of the blue, and found us and kind of freaked out."

My mom settled herself back in her chair. "Is Sunil all right?"

"I don't know."

"You look like you want to punch something," my dad muttered. He tossed me a throw pillow.

I let it bounce off me. I didn't even try to catch it. "Funny. Ha ha."

My mom got up and came over. "I'm sorry. Is their dad as much of a jerk as I think he is?"

"Oh yeah."

"Poor Sunil."

"Yeah," I said, and suddenly the anger turned into heavy emotion and I scrunched my face up, trying not to cry. But it was hopeless. Dysphoria and anger and frustration swirled in my gut as tears fell and my mom wrapped me into a hug.

"Hey, come on. It's going to be okay."

"Why is everything so goddamn hard," I sniffed against her chest, clearing my throat and fighting the tears. I knew it was a toxic way to think, but the times that I couldn't bottle my emotions were when I felt like I was less of a man. And I hated that.

"I don't have an answer for that, Dominic," Mom said softly. "Only that it will get better."

"You don't know that."

"There are some shitty things that come with being an adult, Dominic. But one of the good things is that you have more freedom to do what you want, and to live the way you want, and to love the way you want."

She held me close until I pulled away and wiped my face with the back of my hand.

"Who's winning?" I asked, glancing at the Scrabble board.

"Who do you think?" my dad asked, sighing.

I puffed a sad laugh. "Good job, Mom. Don't you dare back down."

My dad narrowed his eyes at me, then laid some tiles down.

"T-R-A-I-T-O-R for seven points." he said.

18 The Runaway

I WAS WORRIED ABOUT SUNIL. I sat downstairs with my parents for a bit, hoping for a text or something, just to tell me they were okay. After about an hour I sent them a text.

Dom: hey

Dom: are you okay

No response. I started to get really worried. I didn't think their dad would murder them or anything ghoulish like that, but what did I know? Why hadn't they texted?

I went outside to stare at the ocean and worry more. I gazed at the cottage beside ours. There were only a few lights on inside, none upstairs.

The door pushed open slowly, as if the person was being careful.

I stiffened, but soon I could see that it was Sunil, a purple backpack slung over their shoulder, carrying a small black suitcase with wheels so it wouldn't make any noise.

Oh shit.

"Sunil," I said in a stage whisper.

Their head jerked and they saw me. "Hey."

"What are you doing?"

"Sorry, Dominic. I need to get out of here."

"Wait. Sunil, you can't just take off. Come over to our place for a bit."

"I don't want to get your parents in the middle of this."

"Where's your dad?"

"He's upstairs, asleep. I called an Uber to take me to the Halifax airport. I'm going home."

No, no, no.

"You're . . . you're leaving? Tonight?" My throat felt like it might close up.

"I can't do this anymore."

Anger at Sunil's dad, frustration at the situation, and a strong protective instinct took over.

"I'll come with you. You're not going by yourself. I can help you pay for the Uber. Did you call your mom?"

"I'll call her when I get to the airport. When I tell her what's been going on, I know she'll get me a spot on a flight."

I looked at my cottage, where my parents were inside playing board games. Then I looked at Sunil.

They checked their phone. "My Uber's going to be here in fifteen minutes. I'm meeting them in front of the Sand Dunes Grill."

"Okay," I said, holding my hand out for the suitcase.

"What?"

"Give me the suitcase. You've got your backpack.

I'll wait with you."

They handed me the suitcase and we made our way in the dark to the Sand Dunes Grill. The restaurant was lit up inside with a scatter of late-evening customers.

"I just need the washroom. Don't go anywhere." I ducked inside to use the bathroom, the diners giving me curious glances as I went through and into the Men's. A guy was just finishing up at the urinal. He zipped up and only glanced at me benignly as he passed by to get to the sink. After he'd washed his hands and dried them, he left. I went into a stall and took care of business.

I wasn't used to doing things like this, especially without telling my parents. I would tell them, just not right away. Because I didn't want them in the middle of this either.

When I went back outside, Sunil was sitting on their suitcase, looking at their phone.

"I'm really sorry," Sunil muttered when they saw me. They looked exhausted but also determined. "I was having a great time." They waved their hand in the direction of the cottages. "I just can't deal with him anymore."

"I get it," I said. "I know he's your dad but he seems like a dick." I took a seat on the curb. "I'm coming to the airport with you."

They didn't even protest. "Thanks. I was nervous about taking an Uber that far on my own."

"Yeah, well, there's two of us now."

"Will your parents be mad?"

"Probably. But they're not gonna leave me stranded, either."

"True. It must be nice to have reliable parents."

"I never realized how nice until now."

★★★

Our Uber driver's name was Ibrahim. He asked why we were going to Halifax at this time of the night and Sunil calmly replied that we were heading back to Toronto on an early morning flight.

"You look a little young to be travelling by yourselves," Ibrahim said, checking his phone.

"It's on my dad's account. He knows where I am and he'll get a notification of this trip."

    SUMMER WITH SUNIL

I tried to keep a poker face at this blatant lie. Although maybe it wasn't a lie. Maybe I'd misunderstood. I leaned in to whisper in Sunil's ear. "Is that true?"

"Partly. He'll get a notification but he won't see it until morning. His phone's on silent at night."

"Thank god."

"Yeah."

We were quiet then, and I slipped my hand into theirs. They gazed at me and squeezed my fingers, like they had in the SUV on the way to Digby.

"Thanks for coming with," they said.

"You're welcome. I wish you weren't leaving."

"I know."

We sat together in the back of the Uber and watched the trees and flashes of ocean through the darkness.

I got a text from my mom asking why I wasn't back halfway into the trip, and I texted back saying that Sunil was upset and I was with them, which wasn't a lie.

She must have assumed their dad had left and we were alone in their cottage because she didn't ask anything else. I felt kind of awful because I knew that when she did find out I'd taken an Uber to Halifax with Sunil she and Dad would be furious, especially because now they'd have to drive out to get me. But I couldn't let Sunil do this alone. I only hoped that when I explained my reasoning, they'd understand.

Sunil called their mom from the Halifax airport. She was upset but more furious at Sunil's dad after Sunil explained about being left at the cottage on their own. After some texting back and forth she was able to forward them a ticket for a flight to Toronto the next morning. Sunil passed their phone to me and I took it with wide eyes.

"Hello?"

"Hello, Dominic. This is Prisha, Sunil's mother. I want to thank you from the bottom of my heart for being with Sunil. Do your parents know where you are?"

"Yep. Nice to meet you." I shrugged at the look Sunil gave me. They'd know as soon as I finished talking to Sunil's mom.

"That's good. I appreciate you helping my Sunil. We'll have to have you out to Toronto to visit very soon!"

"I'd love that. Thanks."

I gave the phone back to Sunil and called my parents. It was about eleven and my mom picked up the phone, laughing at something my dad was saying.

"Dominic. What's up?"

"Um . . ." I said. Now I was scared to tell her where I was.

"Did Sunil's dad come back?" she said, in a sober tone.

"No. I mean, he's still there. But we're not." I put a hand to my forehead as Sunil looked on with concern.

"What?" she said, her voice suddenly cold. "*Where* are you?"

"Mom, don't get mad. Please. We're safe."

Now it was my dad. "Dominic. Where the hell are you?"

"Hi, Dad. I'm at the Halifax airport. We took an Uber. Sunil's mom got them a flight back to Toronto in the morning."

There was a long silence. I could hear my mom saying my dad's name.

"Jesus Christ. Dominic, I —"

"I'm really sorry. I didn't want Sunil to go alone."

"It's fine, Doreen. They're at the airport in Halifax," my dad said. Except the tone of his voice indicated he didn't think it was actually fine.

"WHAT!" I heard Mom say.

"Dad, I had to go with Sunil."

"They took an Uber. Sunil's going home on a flight in the morning," Dad said.

"Oh my god," my mom said. Now she was on the phone again. "You took an Uber to Halifax? Dominic! We could have driven you . . ."

"Sunil's dad doesn't know and I don't want you and Dad in the middle of this."

"Oh my god," she said again.

I felt so bad. Sunil took my hand.

"Mom, we're safe. There are lots of people here. Everything's fine."

"Everything's fine? For Heaven's sake, Dominic!"

Now my dad had the phone again. "We're coming to get you."

"I'm staying with Sunil until their flight leaves at ten a.m. So, you might as well get some sleep and come in the morning." I squeezed my eyes shut and waited for the explosion.

But my dad was remarkably calm when he spoke after a short pause. "Okay, that makes sense."

"Mark!" my mom said.

"Doreen, they're at the airport. I can't think of a safer place."

"Dominic, you'd better not do anything like this without telling us again!" my mom spoke into the phone.

"I won't. I promise."

All I heard was her breathing for a second. Her voice was a little more tempered when she spoke again. "Is Sunil all right?"

"Yes. They're happy now that they spoke to their

mom and have a flight booked."

"Okay. That's good." She took a moment to calm down a bit more. "You'll be sad to see them go."

"Yeah," I said. I didn't want to tell her how much.

"All right. We'll see you in the morning. Call if there's any problem."

"Yep. We'll be fine."

"All right." She gave an anxious little laugh. "I guess you wanted to show sixteen out with a bang?"

"What?"

"Did you forget? Tomorrow's your birthday."

"Oh damn."

She snorted. "I should know."

"Ha ha. Was motherhood everything you dreamed?"

"Not exactly. And especially not right at this moment, Dominic. But I wouldn't trade it for anything. Love you."

"Love you, too."

The Goodbye

"DO YOU MIND if I rest my head in your lap?" Sunil said with a yawn.

"Of course not."

I checked my phone. It was just after two in the morning. I was kinda sleepy but honestly, more buzzed than anything. I wasn't used to having wild adventures like this. It was exciting and new and I felt like an adult. I liked that feeling.

I also liked being like this with Sunil. I stroked

their hair while they tried to fall asleep.

"Dominic," they said after a little bit.

"Yeah?"

"I've never known anyone like you."

"What do you mean?"

"Like, you know who you are and you don't actually care what anyone else thinks."

"Yeah, I do. I just pretend I don't."

We were quiet for a bit. Then I tapped the tip of Sunil's nose.

"Hey, guess what?"

"What?"

"It's my birthday."

They sat up and stared at me, with their mouth hanging open. "Today? Today's your birthday?"

I smiled. "Yeah."

"Oh, man. Now I'm really sorry to have to leave . . ."

I sighed. "It's okay. I already feel more mature. I guess I can handle it."

"Well . . . happy birthday, Dominic."

"Thanks, Sunil."

They reached for my hand. I gave it to them and they snuggled it to their chest and went to sleep.

At eight in the morning, my parents texted that they planned to be at the airport around ten-thirty.

Dad: **That way you can say your goodbyes in private.**

I blinked, overcome.

Dom: **Thank you.**

Okay, it was official. I had the best parents.

In the morning, while Sunil guarded their bags, I went and got some donuts and coffees. The airport was busier now and Sunil would have to go through security in about half an hour. They'd checked in online and touched base with their mom. I wouldn't be able to join them in the pre-boarding lounge.

"I'm going to miss you, Dominic," Sunil said, sipping their coffee. We'd inhaled our donuts and I'd offered to get Sunil a sandwich to take for their lunch, but they'd declined.

"I can't believe you have to go, but I get it."

"This thing with my dad. I'm pretty sure whatever relationship we used to have is over."

"Fair. I'm sorry."

They shrugged. "We can't all have two amazing parents like yours. At least I have my mom."

"Yeah."

"I know we just started getting . . . closer," Sunil said. "But seeing as we're going to be apart for a while, do you want to go back to being friends, for now?"

I felt a lump in my throat. "Yeah. I guess that makes sense."

"Really good friends," Sunil said. "Like, the best. With the possibility of benefits?" they said with a cheeky smile. "At some point in the future?"

"Friends with benefits?" I said, skeptical. "I was kind of hoping for more."

"You're such a romantic."

"Yeah. When I'm with you I am."

When it was time for them to go, we hugged and I held onto them with a fierceness I hadn't even known I was capable of.

"Text me from the lounge."

"Okay."

            SUMMER WITH SUNIL

"And when you get to Toronto."

"Okay."

"And Sunil . . ." I brushed the hair back from their forehead. "Maybe call me once in a while?"

"I'm going to call you so much. You'll literally be telling me to stop."

"Never."

"Bye, Dominic. Don't let the bed bugs bite."

"Bye, Sunil. Don't ever mention bed bugs again."

They gave me a smile full of regret and then went through the gate.

I waited for my parents in the spot I'd shared with Sunil all night, missing them like mad already and realizing how truly wild the past fourteen hours had been. When I saw my parents approaching from the entrance, it was actually kind of amusing. I could tell they were mad, but trying not to *look* mad, which gave them both very matter-of-fact expressions. I'd never seen my dad's face twitch so much when he said, "Good morning, Dominic."

"Good morning, Dad." I tried not to smile. "I'm really sorry."

"Did Sunil get off all right?" my mom asked, coming close and putting her arm around me like I was her bestie and not her child.

"Yeah."

"Was it hard to say goodbye?"

And suddenly everything caught up to me and I turned into her embrace and started sobbing like a baby.

"Mom," I said, and she hugged me closer.

"Well, I suppose this is a learning opportunity," my dad said.

"Not now, Mark," my mom said. "Let's just go."

My dad drove in silence, while my mom looked out the window at the scenery.

Finally, she spoke.

"Feeling better?" she asked. We'd stopped for breakfast and now I was feeling the effect of a night without sleep.

"Yeah. I'm tired."

"I bet. Look," she said, turning in her seat. "Next time you want to do something this radical, shoot me a text first? Maybe we could have figured something out."

"Sure."

"Your mother and I are getting older, and we do have some life experience. We also don't need more stress," Dad said.

"I know."

He continued, "But . . . we're proud to see you stepping up for someone. Especially someone as adrift as Sunil."

"Thanks."

"I only hope their mom is a better parent than their dad," Mom added.

"She is. From what Sunil's said."

"Good," Mom said.

I laid my head against the window and drifted off to sleep with Samara Joy in my ears and Sunil's dark brown eyes in my thoughts.

★★★

The rest of my summer vacation was pretty boring, except for the daily texts and calls shared with Sunil. They made it back to Toronto and they said I was so in the good books with their mom, which made me happy.

We flew back to Ottawa at the end of August and I started to get ready for school to start the following week.

It was strange to be getting ready to start Grade Twelve. I missed Sunil, but we texted every day and FaceTimed a lot. I even introduced them to my friends over the phone. Mostly to prove I wasn't making the whole thing up.

I went to Toronto over the March Break that year, and again in the summer. Sunil introduced me to their mom and their friends, and showed me all around the Big Smoke, taking me to all the coolest places. We went to Ripley's Aquarium and complained about all the little kids and strollers, but had a great time. Sunil's mom took us to a Blue Jay's game.

Neither of us were sports fans, but Sunil's mom was, and she bought us hot dogs and drinks and popcorn, and we had a blast, watching the players in their tight pants. Sunil's mom rolled her eyes at us but then she agreed that was one of the best parts of going to a game.

Sunil didn't talk about their dad. When I asked about him, they said the two of them didn't have much contact anymore, and that they were never going to go on a trip with him again. I couldn't blame them, but I was glad that circumstances had led us to meet this summer.

EPILOGUE
The Reunion

"WHERE DID THEY SAY they'd meet us?" my dad asked as we drove onto the University of Ottawa campus.

"They're supposed to be at the Marchand building."

I could hardly contain my excitement. But it almost didn't seem real. I kept expecting some text saying that, no, Sunil had changed their plans.

I heard a familiar voice call my name.

I turned around and saw Sunil across the street,

standing with their mom, hefting a huge duffle bag and glancing at the cars to see if they could get across. Their hair was shorter, but curlier.

As my dad uttered words of caution, I weaved between the traffic jam of cars bringing new students to the university residences to get to Sunil. We hugged each other as if it had been years and not only a few weeks since we'd seen each other.

"Can you believe it?" they said. "I'm here! In Ottawa!"

"I know. I can't believe you gave up Toronto for me!"

"Meh. Toronto's noisy and polluted. Here, I've got a view of the Rideau Canal, and you." Sunil's deep brown eyes brimmed with emotion as they gazed at me and I couldn't stop smiling. They were wearing black skinny jeans with a unicorn t-shirt and a pink fluffy sweater, plus a new pair of black Chelsea boots.

I'd put on the U of Ottawa T-shirt that had been in my welcome bag and a pair of cargo jeans, with my army boots. When Sunil and I had both been accepted to the University of Ottawa for our undergraduate degrees, it seemed like fate was sending us a message. Still, I hadn't pressured Sunil to come. I'd wanted them to choose the best university for their degree. But they had registered here and I was totally thrilled about it. We held each other's gazes for a long time, speaking a silent truth that was only waiting for the right moment.

Sunil's mom grabbed a bag out of her car and shut the door.

"Dominic! How are you?"

I broke away from Sunil's intense gaze and turned to their mom. "Good! How are you, Prisha?"

"I'm excited to get Sunil settled. And then the three of us can go out for dinner. How about that? Your parents can join us if they'd like."

"We'd love to," my dad said, "but we promised our daughter we'd go to her concert. So, we'll have to take a raincheck."

"Of course. But I can have Dominic?"

"You can have Dominic." Dad turned to me.

　　　　SUMMER WITH SUNIL

"I'm going to head back."

"Okay, Dad. Thanks."

Prisha looked at her watch. "Dominic, if you can help us get Sunil's things to their room, I'll go grab some coffees and donuts."

"Sure!"

The halls of the residence building were full of kids our age hauling bags and small items to their new dorm rooms. Sunil's was in the middle of the hall, halfway between the common area and the washrooms.

"Communal washrooms. That'll take some getting used to," they said.

"At least it's co-ed. Everyone uses the same toilets, no matter what gender they are."

"In theory, that sounds great. I'm going to miss sharing one with only my mom, or better yet, when I had my very own at the cottage." They sighed. "You know, I actually have fond memories of that place, thanks to you."

"Well, this is definitely smaller. And the view isn't as nice." I gazed around us at the cramped room that would be Sunil's home for the next eight months. "I wish my parents could have paid for me to live in residence, at least for *one* year."

"You've got it pretty good with your parents."

"Sure. But you get to do the whole adult thing and control your own life."

"Don't forget I've done that, and it's not as glamorous as they say."

"Well, you won't be lonely. Because I plan to hang out with you so much, you're going to get sick of me."

"That will never happen."

"I'm going to remind you that you said that."

"I'm okay with it."

"Welcome to Ottawa, Sunil. 'The City that Fun Forgot!'"

"I'm gonna bring so much fun. You'll never get rid of me now."

I threw my head back and laughed.

Sunil reached out and took my hand, pulling me forward. We stood so close I could see the little flecks of gold in their brown eyes.

"Dominic Dunn. Would you go steady with me again, now that we're living in the same place?"

"Well, I'll have to let all the others down gently, I guess," I said.

Sunil knew it was a joke, and they rolled their eyes. Neither of us had dated anyone, even though we'd had opportunities.

I continued. "Of course, I do."

"I want to kiss you," Sunil breathed.

"Then do it," I said. It was two years since we'd met, and I think I'd loved them since that summer.

Sunil's lips landed on mine and a host of angels sang.

Well, not actually, but it felt good and right and it was about damn time.

ACKNOWLEDGEMENTS

With much thanks to my mother, Charlotte, who was born and grew up in Liverpool, Nova Scotia, and who passed unexpectedly in 2016. And to my father, Chris, who drove us from Ottawa to Liverpool many times to visit. The unparalleled beauty of Queens County, Nova Scotia, is with me, still.

I'd also like to thank my children (19 and 17), who give me inspiration and joy each day.